Rumble in Rio

Steve Higgs

Contents

Prologue

Xavier Silvestre watched the ship, scanning the crowd until he found her. It took longer than he expected because she was not where he thought she would be.

Patricia Fisher ought to have left the ship via the royal suite's exit. Located forward and well away from the general passenger exit set amidships, the VIPs had an awning to stand under if it chose to rain or indeed if the sun proved to be particularly fierce as it was today. Town cars, or one might call them limousines, decorated with the cruise line's livery were then at hand to whisk their top paying guests to wherever it is they wanted to go.

Patricia Fisher chose to use neither exit.

Nor did she leave when the rest of the passengers disembarked. Silvestre took it all in his stride, refusing to let the enticingly mysterious woman annoy him. He was above such things; in control and one step ahead.

He could not know with any certainty where the English sleuth would head once she came ashore, but knowing what he did, Silvestre was willing to bet she would find the lure of the Museum of Brazil too great to resist.

He had posed as a professor who worked there ... used to work there, for Professor Noriega was dead. Silvestre killed him to ensure secrets remained just that. Professor Noriega was the world's leading authority on a Spanish treasure ship called the San José. Supposedly sunk three hundred years ago, Silvestre believed the ship and its cargo were stolen by the crew and hidden. Something had then befallen the men behind it for only a few pieces of the treasure had ever surfaced.

Xavier Silvestre had made it his life's work to find the location of the San José's treasure and that had led him here. A man had been found on board the Aurelia, the giant cruise ship that filled his binoculars. His name was Finn Murphy, and he was dead just like the professor. Silvestre hadn't killed him though; Carlos Ramirez, a common con-man and thief, had committed that crime.

Ramirez thought he could rob Murphy who approached him to sell some uncut gemstones he'd found. Ramirez didn't get the stones, but he took a dagger from Murphy's body and that sealed his own fate - the dagger bore the crest of a family who travelled and died on the San José.

Finn Murphy had found the treasure.

Now Silvestre's only link to what Murphy knew lay with the English woman. She might know nothing, but if she did, Xavier Silvestre would extract it from her. Plus, she had the gems and he wanted them. Just to hold something that had been hidden for so long …

When his binoculars finally spotted the elusive woman, Silvestre was surprised to find her accompanying a crate as it was wheeled off the ship.

Had Murphy found more treasure than Silvestre first believed? The San José carried many hundreds of tons of gold, jewels, and other precious items, but as he held his breath and squinted at the crate to see what it might contain. Something moved inside.

It was livestock, not treasure.

It didn't matter, Silvestre silently assured himself. In fact, it was better if all she possessed were a few uncut gems. If word got out that the San José had been found, it would spark a treasure hunt the like of which the world had never seen.

No, he needed to carefully extract whatever information Patricia Fisher knew, recover the gems he knew she possessed, and silence her. Permanently. Only once she was dead and the trail to the San José was only being pursued by him would he be able to fully relax.

Tracking her movements along the quayside, Silvestre's heart skipped a beat when he saw her meeting with local law enforcement officers. Was she handing over the jewels to them? Did she somehow know more than he believed she could?

Watching, his heart hammering in his chest, Xavier Silvestre held his breath.

Goodbye to a Nemesis

J ermaine's voice invaded my thoughts. "The police are here, Madam."

I twisted to face the sound of approaching cars as their tyres crunched slowly across the asphalt and I turned to nod my head at Lieutenant Commander Baker.

Crimes committed in international waters are confusing things. The person accused of the crime comes from one country, the crimes have been committed in another, or possibly in a location not designated to any country. The ship is registered in and obeys the laws of yet another nation, and we have to hand our prisoner off to the authorities in whichever country we make port.

Regardless of the confusing nature surrounding the transfer of suspected criminals from our brig to the custody of local law enforcement, the rules governing the how and why are well established.

We had a person on board who needed to be sent for trial and though technically she would be innocent until proven guilty, there was no doubt in anyone's mind that she was insanely criminal.

Baker brought her out of the ship sandwiched between him and his oversized Austrian counterpart, Lieutenant Schneider. Flanking them were Lieutenant's Deepa Bhukari and Anders Pippin.

Four armed security officers from the ship's team for just one woman because she really was that dangerous.

Bending a little at the waist to look inside the crate, I said, "I'll be back in a moment, Buddy. I need to take care of this first."

Buddy, a Gibraltar Rock Ape, flipped a middle finger at me and grinned.

Angelica Howard-Box glared at me from the moment she stepped out from the shadows inside the ship and never once broke her stare or even blinked as I made my way toward her. I had attended school with her, but strenuously avoided employing the word 'schoolfriend' because Angelica hated me even back then.

"The transfer paperwork is in order?" I asked, my question aimed at Lieutenant Commander Baker though I continued to return Angelica's gaze.

"Yes, Mrs Fisher."

I nodded, feeling a little overwhelmed and wondering if there was anything I ought to say before they took her away. She had blighted my life for years, though never more so than since I inadvertently gained the favour of a Maharaja. Sneaking on board the Aurelia weeks ago, Angelica had waged a guerrilla war against me, doing everything she could to ruin my life only to fail miserably and in turn ruin her own.

I could not imagine how she could hope to avoid serious jail time.

The Rio police were waiting to take her into custody. They would hold her until she was transported back to the UK if, indeed, that was where her trial would take place. It wasn't any of my concern.

Turning away, I paused. I did have a final thing I wanted to say.

Facing her once more, I sucked in a deep lungful or air, and said, "I'm sorry it came to this, Angelica. I truly wish you could have been happy in your own life."

Her eyes narrowed just a fraction. It wasn't enough to interrupt the seething hatred they displayed, but that vanished a moment later when she tipped her head back and laughed.

A tirade of abuse and unprintable curse words was what I expected, and the guffaws were not only inappropriate to the situation but indicative of just how unhinged she had become.

Patiently, I waited for them to subside, but that was not what happened. Whether deliberate or opportune, Angelica had thrown

Schneider and Baker off guard with her deranged laughter. It stopped abruptly when she twisted to angle herself at me.

Kicking out with mad viciousness, Angelica would have landed a blow to my midriff had Jermaine not been close to hand. My six-foot four-inch Jamaican butler deftly parried her kick with an almost lazy left hand.

There was to be no follow up. Baker and Schneider seized her instantly, yanking her away from me as the litany of expected insults filled the air.

"This isn't over, Patricia Fisher! I'm going to kill you if it's the last thing I ever do. You will rot in hell for your sins!"

I got an apologetic grimace from Baker as they led the struggling woman away.

That should have been that, but I guess that's just not how my life works.

"Good riddance, you psychopath!" yelled Gloria, appearing from inside the ship where she had been waiting with her grandson, Ensign Sam Chalk. Gloria is in her eighties and on board the ship to look after Sam. Sam is my assistant and has Downs. Sam is utterly brilliant and a constant joy to be around. Gloria ... not so much.

Her comment was closely followed by two eggs.

The first struck the back of Angelica's head, smashing upon contact. The second missed.

Or rather, it missed Angelica, for it did not miss the senior police officer sent to collect our prisoner.

I heard Gloria say, "Oops," when it hit his chin and went splat all over the front of his uniform.

Entertained by our antics or possibly just wanting to join in, Buddy started going ape in his cage. The Gibraltar Rock Ape, a stowaway passenger since we docked there a week ago, was finally on his way home. Like Angelica, there were people coming to collect him.

Before he could start flinging anything of his own making – he was known for doing so - a cover was lowered over his cage by the unlucky members of crew assigned to look after him.

Gloria had retreated inside the ship, leaving the Rio police staring at Sam. Frozen to the spot, he said, "Um."

Hanging my head, though only for a moment, I almost elbowed Barbie, my size zero, gym instructor friend from California. She was giggling into her hands and failing to hide how amusing she found the situation.

The Rio police looked like they were going to draw their sidearms when I chose to intervene.

"Goodness, I'm so sorry about that." I didn't have to fake the colour rising in my cheeks. "My friends and I have been put through the mill by this woman."

The captain, if I was able to interpret his rank insignia correctly, had stopped staring at the mess on his shirt and was glaring at the ship until I spoke.

"This is assault on a police officer, Mrs Fisher. It is Mrs Fisher, yes?"

I pulled a face that hopefully expressed how bad I felt about the state of his uniform.

"Yes. Yes, that's me. Please send me the cleaning bill," I requested, rolling straight over the part about his assault. "A most unfortunate accident."

I wasn't winning him over, that much was clear from his thunderous expression. He wasn't happy about it, but what was he going to do? Arrest an old lady?

"I was aiming for the crazy woman!" Gloria's voice rang out from inside the ship's hull.

"I'm not crazy!" screeched Angelica, kinda disproving her own point. Bucking against the men holding her in place, she refused to calm down and continued to hurl abuse my way even as they led her to a waiting van.

One of the officers signed for the transfer and I thought that was going to be it, but Captain Santoro – I was right about his rank – wasn't content to let things lie.

"The person who assaulted me, are they passenger or crew?"

Tilting my head as I tried to gauge his intentions, I said, "It hardly matters. It was an egg, and it wasn't intentionally aimed at you."

His gaze swung around and down to pierce my eyes with his.

"There is a zero-tolerance policy for assault on police officers in Rio de Janeiro, Mrs Fisher. It is not up to me whether I let this incident go or not. Now that your prisoner has been successfully transferred into my custody, I must insist you hand over the person who threw the egg."

"She's in her eighties," I remarked, doing nothing to hide the criticism in my tone.

"And yet quite young and capable enough to cause trouble. Her age is of no concern. Her lack of respect for my authority is."

"She was aiming at Angelica!" I felt like stamping my foot.

"Mrs Fisher, I tire of this discussion. I am not asking your permission and my tolerance thus far is based only upon a willingness to cooperate. That willingness is about to evaporate. Must I enforce my authority and take the transgressor?"

Okay, so here's a thing. Not so very long ago I wouldn't have dreamed of arguing with anyone. I was a timid, mousey woman with zero confidence and a habit of hiding from life in general. Not so much anymore.

In the half second between Captain Santoro delivering his ultimatum, and me reacting, he had nodded his head at two of his officers, dispatching them in the direction of the ship to fetch Gloria from her hiding place.

"Halt!" The power and authority behind the single word was enough to make everyone stop moving. That it came from me shocked a few people.

Barbie, a few feet away in a wheelchair to keep weight off an injured leg, gasped, "Patty."

Captain Santoro opened his mouth, and I could tell he was going to shout something.

I got in first.

"You have no authority here, Sir," I challenged, stepping to block his path to the ship. "You are dockside and thus outside of your jurisdiction, Captain Santoro." This was doing nothing for local relations which were important to the cruise line, but I didn't feel like I had a choice. "If you do not back off immediately, I will have my officers take you into custody." I let those words sink in, watching the captain's expression turn from disbelief to anger before I added, "Are we clear?"

No one had drawn their sidearms, but Baker, Schneider, and the others were all poised to do so.

To my great relief, Captain Santoro spat, "This is an outrage!" It was the best response I felt I could hope for and a long way from ordering his men to continue with his previous order.

Speaking calmly, I said, "It is unfortunate that you made this necessary, Captain. There was no need to escalate the situation as you have. I will not, however, mention this in my report which will state the prisoner transfer occurred without incident."

A sneer split his face.

"You can state whatever falsehoods you wish, Mrs Fisher. My report will tell the truth." With another nod of his head, his officers withdrew, doffing their hats as they slid into the patrol cars. "You may have authority here, Mrs Fisher. Out there though," he jinked his head toward the towering landscape that is Rio, "I rule. Think twice before you come ashore."

He gave me no time to retort, not that I had anything in my head that felt worth saying. The door to his car slammed shut, ending the standoff, but also jarring me into action.

Spinning around, I spotted Gloria leaning out of her hiding place once again armed with an egg.

"Noooooooo!" slipped from my lips as time stood still and I watched Sam's gran pull her arm back.

Everyone moved to stop her, but none were close enough and we all knew she was crazy enough to launch another weapon at the departing police cars.

Sam grabbed his gran's arm. He'd been tucked in the shadows with her, probably trying to keep her quiet because she was known for saying precisely what she thought regardless of the consequences.

The egg fell from her grip to smash on the ground.

She said a rude word.

"Gloria," I shook my head and caught my breath. "What were you thinking?"

Indignantly, she replied, "That Angelica got off lightly. And that police officer, well he was just rude. I never meant to hit him with the egg …"

Gloria continued to argue for the next half an hour, ceaselessly pointing out that she wasn't to blame, and that Angelica had it coming. On the last point, I agreed.

It was my first time in Rio de Janeiro and the ship was to be here for two days. It was breakfast when the first passengers started to depart the ship, bound for all manner of different destinations though many would simply explore the great city. I was desperate to join them, but duty had to come first, so three hours after everyone else, with Angelica now someone else's problem and Buddy the Gibraltar Rock Ape on his way back home, I was finally heading into the city.

Funny thing is Captain Santoro's words of warning never once entered my head.

Dorothy and Pals

Looking like Dorothy and pals skipping down the yellow-brick road, I was accompanied by Jermaine, Barbie, and Sam as we made our way into Rio. Jermaine was out of his butler's garb for once, and dressed in bright blue shorts and a pink vest in deference to the Brazilian climate. Barbie, the almost six-foot blonde goddess opted for a simple, red halter neck dress and pristine white running shoes. Okay, so she was in a wheelchair and could only wear one shoe, but her outfit shone like the sun, nonetheless.

Sam had a yellow, designer brand polo shirt that was his current favourite above dress shorts and deck shoes. Knowing I had people to meet and impress, I wore a lightweight jacket by Chanel – a designer that suits women my age and wore that over a fitted white shirt and jeans. I was a little warm in the midday sun, but inside the museum – our destination – I expected to be comfortable.

Gloria had gone ashore with friends her own age. We get lots of pairs or even groups of older women travelling with us on the Aurelia. Many of them are widows and they gravitate toward each other. I hoped she would stay out of trouble.

The rest of my security detachment – the five officers, most recently increased from four by the addition of Molly Lawrie, a new member of crew and my former housemaid, were doing their own thing at my insistence.

Baker and Bhukari had only married a few weeks ago and since their honeymoon had worked almost every day. Molly and Anders Pippin were pretending they were not dating even though a blind person could tell they were. The young couple made a point of not arriving anywhere together. Ever. When people made plans, they always had excuses why they couldn't partake, and their reasons never once aligned as they would if they had not rehearsed their answers in advance.

Like the others, I kept my nose out of their business and hoped their relationship wouldn't implode in a way that would impact the team's cohesion.

We stopped for lunch as it was very much that time of day, Barbie and Jermaine leading our foursome to a place serving what they assured us would be the best barbecued meat we had ever eaten.

They were not wrong.

While we ate, conversation turned to the next item on our agenda.

Barbie asked, "What do you think we will find, Patty?"

She was referring to the Museum of Brazil and the trail of bizarre clues that led us there. Two weeks ago, the body of an unknown man was discovered deep in the hull of the ship where no passenger ought to ever find themselves.

He'd been murdered, there was no question about that as the knife that killed him was still stuck in his chest. In the man's gut was a small fortune in uncut gems and as mysterious as that was, it paled by comparison when we found where he had been sleeping.

The chance discovery of his grubby backpack and tatty sleeping bag led to his passport so we were at least able to identify him and repatriate the body. Finn Murphy, an Irishman, was a stowaway with a big bag of secrets. He also had an actual big bag filled with priceless gold coins and precious gemstones.

The mystery begged to be solved, but other ... shall we say dramas, got in the way. Angelica was just part of that.

There were no real clues to lead us in any direction until Professor Noriega from the Museum of Brazil arrived onboard the Aurelia to quiz us about the uncut jewels we found. You might be questioning how he could possibly know about them, and the answer is that Angelica hacked my computer and made it look like I was a fame hungry media hound trying to get my name in the papers.

Once the report I'd written for my own purposes was out there, there was of course, no taking it back.

Here's the thing though – Professor Noriega died a week before we met him. No, it's not a case for Tempest and the Blue Moon team. What I mean is that the person we met was an imposter. Did he kill the real professor so he could take the man's place? Well, that I don't know, but as I dabbed politely at my lips with a napkin and set my plate to one side, it was something I intended to find out.

Then I was going to figure out why.

The Museum

To my mind the Museum of Brazil looks quite a lot like the Natural History Museum in London. It's huge, it's old, and both buildings bear a sort of foreboding silence as if they know what treasures they possess and are jealously watching the people daring to enter lest they attempt to take something other than knowledge away with them.

Due to a little research, Barbie had been able to make contact with another professor, a man called Bruno Baccarin, so we were expected and had an appointment to see him. Like Professor Noriega, Professor Baccarin worked in the marine antiquities department of the museum.

The email she sent him was speculative and omitted the part about our visit from a man posing as his dead colleague. Instead, she carefully outlined the uncut gems and coins we now had in our possession, but without sending him pictures though he did request them.

The carefully dangled carrot ensured he would see us.

The cruise line limousine dropped us in front of the museum where a line of visitors were filing through the grand entrance. It looked to be a fifteen or twenty-minute wait to get inside, but we were not going in with the public. Following Professor Baccarin's instructions, we turned left, kept the museum to our right and walked around the side to find the staff entrance.

We had to pass through a security gate where a guard in a small hut checked my name against a list. Satisfied, he let us through, Jermaine wheeling Barbie with Sam and me leading the way. Passing beneath old stone arches and into a courtyard, we skirted a carpark, following a path until we finally found a sign pointing us to reception.

As one might expect, the public front of the museum hides an academic hub at the back. Visiting scholars from around the world would come to inspect artefacts and experts would meet to discuss new theories. I knew this from looking at the academic section of the museum's website which I accessed to look at a photograph of the late Professor Noriega.

Striding confidently into the building just a few minutes before our appointment with Professor Baccarin, I expected to be asked to wait for someone to collect us. However, when we arrived at the reception desk, the lady working there had a surprise for us.

"Professor Geller wishes to meet you first, Mrs Fisher," she explained, tapping a button on her phone to connect a call. "Professor Geller is the head of the museum."

It was not what I expected, but had no reason to argue.

The lady, a dark-skinned beauty in her fifties with just a touch of grey creeping through her lustrous black hair, spoke into the microphone of her headset, rattling out a question in Portuguese. The only part of it I understood was my name when she said it, but I knew both Barbie and Jermaine spoke at least some Portuguese.

The lady nodded her head in response to whatever the person at the end told her, ended the call, and said, "Professor Geller is on his way down."

Less than a minute later, a thin man in an old suit appeared on the stairs to our right. He was coming down them at speed, jogging almost and was coming right for us.

"Here he is now," the reception lady let us know.

Angling my feet in his direction, I took a step forward to shake his hand and greet him. That the head of the museum had taken time out from his day to not only meet with me, but chose to collect me in person impressed me. I could only guess why it was that he felt the need to speak with me, but expected I would find out soon enough.

"Mrs Fisher," he hallooed enthusiastically as he drew near.

Barbie hissed from the corner of her mouth, "It looks like you've got a fan, Patty."

That was exactly how it seemed.

"Call me Patricia, please," I returned his smile.

"Then I am Lino, Patricia," he clutched my right hand between both of his. "Won't you please accompany me back to my office? I will not delay your meeting with Professor Baccarin for very long. It's so rare to have a celebrity visit our museum."

I felt heat rush to my cheeks. "Well, I would hardly call myself a celebrity ..."

"Oh, nonsense, Patricia. You have been in all the papers."

The professor led us back to the stairs and was about to ascend them when he spotted his mistake. Barbie didn't really need to be in a wheel-chair, but her boyfriend, Dr Hideki Nakamura, insisted her recovery would be swifter if she stayed off her injured ankle. She was doing as she was told and that meant we needed an elevator.

Professor Geller continued to talk about my exploits, those of which he knew about, with gusto as we rose through the old building to his office on the top floor. I assessed his age to be somewhere around seventy-five and noted that he wore no wedding ring. When he shook my hand, I had spotted a Patek Philippe watch on his wrist and from that deduced that he had significantly more money than he needed. Standing a shade over six feet tall, he would have been an inch or two taller fifty years ago and probably considered a giant at the time. The most notable feature though, was his hair. He had some grey around his temples, but for the most part it was a bright coppery colour. In all other respects he looked Brazilian, but his hair declared a mix of racial heritage somewhere in his past.

Exiting the elevator into a hallway lit only by overhead lights and a single window at the far end, we were surrounded by displays of ancient fossils.

"This is my area of expertise," he bragged. "Palaeontology fascinated me from a very early age and when I found a Spinosaurus tooth in a gravel pit at the tender age of eight, I was hooked forever."

Pushing a large wooden door open, he led us into an office with windows looking out across the museum grounds. The room, like the hallway outside, was filled with cabinets displaying fossils.

Seeing my attention drawn to them, he explained, "These are some of my other finds. I'm too old for the digging side of things now, which is a shame, but we have to accept our limitations."

He was yet to explain why he wanted to see me, or why he felt a need to bring us to his office, but playing the patient and polite guest, I did as I knew I should and acted as though interested.

"Did you discover any species yourself?"

My question drew a smile.

"Twelve, Patricia. I was able to identify and name ten new dinosaurs and two flying reptiles. Of course, the technology behind the science has made it so the modern-day fossil hunters find a new species almost every day."

"Really?" I asked, surprised by his statement.

He pumped his eyebrows. "I'm exaggerating, of course, but the influx of new fossils waiting to be examined, categorised, and catalogued has become more than we can handle. They are building up in our store-rooms and there is probably a year's worth of work for a whole team just to catch up." He looked into the distance for a moment, thinking something before snapping back to the present. "My apologies, I've dragged you up here and all I have done is prattle on about my fossils. I should get to the point, shouldn't I?"

Professor Geller relaxed into a chair, indicating that my friends and I should also sit.

Settling into a sturdy yet comfortable armchair, I said, "Yes, Lino, I am pleased to have met you, but I must admit I am curious to hear why you were so keen to make my acquaintance."

Thankfully, he beat around the bush no longer.

"I wanted to ask, in private, what drove you to come here today, Patricia. When I heard of your request to meet with Professor Baccarin, I must confess it sounded alarm bells in my head."

A frown pinched my eyebrows together. "Why alarm bells, Lino?"

He allowed himself a nervous chuckle. "Because one of my colleagues died recently and just a few days later, a well-known sleuth wishes to visit. Do you know something about Professor Noriega's passing? I was assured it was nothing more than a terrible accident. Are you here to investigate? And if so, why?"

So that was the crux of it. Barbie calls me a trouble magnet. I don't like it, but she does have a point. Trouble just occurs wherever I go.

Chewing on my bottom lip, I considered my dilemma. I like to think of myself as an honest person, but I already knew I was about to lie to Professor Geller. It wasn't so much that I wished to hide the truth about the reason for my visit, but the more people I told, the greater the danger of the news spreading.

It was my job to solve Finn Murphy's murder and to add to that was the desire to make sure the treasure he had in his possession went where it was supposed to go. The man posing as Professor Noriega had mentioned a shipwreck and it made sense that coins, which we knew to be three hundred years old, might come from a sunken ship. I knew little of such things, but Finn Murphy's rucksack of treasure, now hidden in my safe on the ship, contained millions of dollars of treasure – easily enough to get people killed. The fewer people I told about it the better. However, I had to tell Professor Geller something.

Smiling, I said, "Did you see the report I published about the stow-away's body found on the Aurelia?" Okay, so I didn't publish it at all, but there was no sense getting into that.

"Yes, I did, Patricia. It sounded very cloak and dagger. He had gem-stones in his stomach, did he not?"

"Indeed he did. I'm afraid I cannot tell you all that I am sure you would like to know; I am investigating that man's murder and cannot discuss an ongoing case." It was another outright lie; I wasn't bound by any such rules. "However, I can tell you the man was on his way here to Rio with the express intent of seeing Professor Noriega. I'm not suggesting Professor Noriega's death is in any way related to the murder on board our cruise ship," I really was, "but I am here to pursue the slim hope that Professor Noriega's close colleague, Professor Baccarin, might know something."

Professor Geller absorbed what I had told him and thought on it for a few seconds before responding.

"Thank you, Patricia. Thank you for telling me what you could. I shall not pester you for further details. Professor Noriega's loss was a terrible blow to this faculty; he was a brilliant man."

Our meeting had run its course and I was keen to move on – I really did have a murder to solve and questions for Professor Baccarin to answer.

"Can you direct us to Professor Baccarin's office?" I requested.

Rising from his chair, the head of the museum reached over to pluck the handset of the phone from his desk. A few words in Portuguese later, he let us know Professor Baccarin's grad student was on his way to collect us.

Inigo Montoya

Ten minutes dragged by, Professor Geller making idle chitchat with me until the sound of approaching feet brought the chance to escape. A moment later, a shockingly handsome young man with a broad smile appeared at the office door. The smile was mostly aimed at Barbie who he had spotted instantly.

Barbie is thirty years my junior, has four inches height advantage and beats me by two cup sizes. If she wasn't so darned nice, she would be very easy to dislike.

"Good morning," he beamed, "I have been sent to collect Patricia Fisher?" His eyes were still fixed on Barbie as he hopefully enquired if he had found the right person and would be able to now enjoy her company for a brief time.

"That's me," I volunteered, narrowing my eyes at the young man when I saw his crestfallen expression.

He recovered quickly. "Good morning, Mrs Fisher," he looked around to take in Jermaine and Sam, lingering once more on Barbie's radiant face, "and companions. My name is Inigo Montoya. I am one of Professor Baccarin's grad students. Please follow me."

When he turned and began to walk away, Barbie remarked on his hooded top.

"Oh, you went to U of C? Which Campus?"

The words emblazoned across his back, which I would not have noticed had she not commented, did indeed proclaim University of California.

Inigo twisted around to look at Barbie, but the excited twinkle his eyes bore just a few moments ago was gone, replace by a slightly haunted look.

"Um, San Diego," he replied, his tone sounding careful.

Barbie squealed, "No way! That's where I went! What year did you graduate?"

Inigo hesitated to give his answer, the rapid eye movement suggesting he was trying to perform mental calculations before he committed to a year.

Again Barbie squealed at his answer, "That was the year after me! I bet we know loads of the same people. I bet we even drank at the same bars. Not that I drank much other than water back then. Ooh, do you know, Sandra Ohmeier? She was definitely in your year. I remember her because she was in my gymnastics squad."

Now, you can call it instinct, or a learned skill ... whichever it was, I knew our guide was lying.

"Um, I was only there for two semesters, I'm afraid. My family had to move and it wasn't possible for me to stay behind. I don't really remember anyone from that time."

It wasn't the words he used, it was the tone and the panicked manner in which he said them. That and his eyes. He was lying.

Barbie fired a few more names at him, convinced they would have some connection, but accepted defeat after five or six 'Nos'. As much as anything, the fact that he hadn't offered to take her for coffee to discuss the matter further was evidence enough he was trying to hide something.

I filed it away to consider later.

We fell into line behind Inigo, allowing the now nervous young man to lead us through the warren of corridors to his boss's office.

Arriving in a new corridor, the walls on both sides were adorned with old oil paintings, a huge fossil Sam identified as a plesiosaur, maps, and all manner of other ageing or ancient artefacts. Built long before anyone would have thought to use glass in abundance to let in light, there were no windows at all save for one right at the end of the hallway and those inset into the doors.

Inigo stopped to knock on a door before turning the handle and entering without waiting for whoever was inside to answer.

Filing in behind him, I saw a small man in his sixties rising from a chair set against a desk by a window. The room itself was filled with books on several wooden bookshelves which bore the look of furniture hewn from trees more than a century ago. The effort of getting them into the building and into place on the third floor was a feat in itself. I could only guess what they might weigh.

Elsewhere around the room I spotted models of ships, rolls of parchment and long cardboard tubes that could contain charts or maps. There were shelves of artefacts, most of which I could not identify though I was able to pick out and name a brass sextant.

On the wall by the desk were a series of photographs showing the man who was now advancing toward us. He was younger in the pictures and had a head of thick black hair. The photographs had to be close to twenty years old and were of a diving expedition where ancient treasures were being recovered from the deep.

"Mrs Fisher, your name precedes you. I am Professor Bruno Baccarin. Welcome to my humble office."

My friends parted, stepping backward as the professor advanced to shake my hand.

"Thank you for agreeing to see us," I felt no need to repeat my own name since he knew who I was. "These are my companions: Jermaine.

Barbie. And Sam." He made a point of shaking their hands in turn, stopping at Barbie.

"The email I received was from you, yes?"

Barbie nodded her head. "It was. We have some items to show you and a few questions to ask about Professor Noriega."

Professor Baccarin nodded his head in understanding and looked to have as many questions of his own.

"Yes, Julio's passing was … he and I were very good friends. We have been through some times together. It pains me that he never got to realise his dream."

"His dream?" I encouraged the professor to explain.

"Please, please, find somewhere to sit." He looked around his own office, pulling a face at the lack of available chairs. "Inigo, help me to tidy some of these research papers, will you?"

Jermaine and Sam offered to help only to be asked they not touch anything.

"It's all organised," Professor Baccarin assured us, then laughed, "Even though you would never be able to tell."

We all waited patiently, but it didn't take very long for the professor and Inigo to clear enough space for the four of us to sit.

"You were telling us that Professor Noriega had a goal he wasn't able to achieve before his death," I nudged Professor Baccarin to continue what he had been saying.

"Yes, sorry. Tenure. Julio was never granted tenure and it was a mystery why Professor Geller continued to overlook him. Or possibly block the appointment. I don't know which it was, but I received mine five years ago."

Sam asked, "What's tenure?" and we all got to listen to Professor Baccarin explain how teachers or lecturers were typically granted a permanent position once they had demonstrated sufficient commitment not only to their institution, but to the academic field of study to which they were dedicated.

"It was the final piece of his academic career and in many ways an insult that he had not been awarded what should have been a formality. Now, how about some coffee?" Professor Baccarin asked, snatching up his own mug from among the paper detritus on his desk. "Inigo, if you please?"

The professor's student took an order for hot beverages, something I did not imagine wanting today, but which felt right at home in the cool environment of the museum. He bustled away, finally leaving us to get down to the business that brought us to his door.

Barbie nudged me before I could get started, leaning in to make sure I was looking in the right direction when she flicked out a finger.

It took me a second to figure out what I was supposed to be seeing.

In one corner of the professor's office, Inigo had an area for his things. I spotted a folder embossed with the U of C logo, a ballcap with the same and a photograph of what appeared to be his graduating year.

That he had lied about his time there had not been missed by my blonde friend.

Leaving it for now – I could not yet perceive a connection between his deception and our business, I turned my attention to Jermaine.

"The coin, sweetie?"

Jermaine had been entrusted to carry the priceless gold coin because of all of us, he was the least likely to have it taken from him. Jermaine was trained to be a butler for one of the ship's royal suites and part of the required skills for the role included years of martial arts expertise.

Basically, my butler is a tall, muscular ninja who could fight a bear and a rhino at the same time and probably come out of the exchange in one piece.

From an inside pocket, Jermaine produced a closed hand, turning it over to reveal the coin with a flourish.

Leaning forward, Profession Baccarin peered at the glinting metal object, his eyebrows dancing until his brain told him precisely what he was looking at.

"Oh, Dios mío!" he squawked, almost falling off his chair as he lunged for the coin. The next few sentences were all in Portuguese, and even if I could speak the language, which I can't, I doubt I would have got any of it because his words blended into one long Portuguesey burble.

Barbie leaned into me. "He keeps saying that it can't be. It can't be. It's not possible. Something about a ship called the San José ..."

She was cut off when the professor, his eyes as big as cooking apples, begged to know, "Where did you get this? Do you have any idea what this means?"

My response was interrupted by an almost silent knock at the door. It opened a moment later, a familiar crockery and spoons on a tray sound coming with it. Our coffee had arrived, but it wasn't being carried by Inigo. In his place, a young woman was carrying the tray.

Holding it awkwardly with one arm so it squashed her breasts in a bid to keep it from spilling, she came into the room and slowly revolved to get the door.

Jermaine got to his feet a fraction quicker than Sam, darting across the room to help the young woman.

She had pale skin highlighted by her black hair and deep brown eyes. Pretty in a girl-next-door kind of way, what struck me most was how sad she looked. Studying her face for a moment longer, I then questioned if I perhaps had it wrong. Maybe it wasn't sadness I was seeing, but fear.

What did she have to fear?

It was at this point that I spotted her name badge.

"Sonia Noriega?" I questioned, watching her face when it shot up to look at me. "Your father was Professor Julio Noriega?"

She didn't answer, but just like Inigo, her eyes gave me the confirmation I needed.

"I'm so sorry for your loss."

"Where is Inigo, Sonia?" Professor Baccarin asked, his tone annoyed.

Sonia's eyes were cast down to the floor when she replied, "He asked me if I could deliver the coffees, Professor. He didn't say why he couldn't do it."

To avoid further questions. The answer echoed in my head, but with Jermaine handing out the coffee and Sonia already backing out the door, I raced to speak with her before she could depart.

"Sonia, is it possible that I can speak with you about your father? I won't need much of your time." I didn't know what I was going to ask her, but the official verdict of misadventure – Professor Noriega had been knocked down and killed in a hit and run accident – was innocent enough until one factored in the man impersonating him a week after his death.

The mystery man found me on board the Aurelia and when I failed to supply him with answers because I was hip deep in solving a case, he chose to attack me with a knife. Whoever he was, he knew more than I did and there was altogether too much coincidence of timing for me to dismiss the possibility that the real professor's accident was nothing of the sort.

"I'm ... I'm sorry. I have to go." She turned away from me and was shocked when I caught her arm.

I let it go just as quickly but my invasion of her personal space had done the trick and I had her attention now.

"Please, Sonia, if you are in danger. If there is anything you need to say and don't know who to trust, please let me help. My name is Patricia Fisher, please look me up." I hoped that would do the trick. If my skull hadn't already been itching, her behaviour would have caused it rightly enough.

She backed away just as Professor Baccarin left his office to join us in the corridor.

"Is everything all right?" he asked, peering over the top of his spectacles.

"I'm sorry," Sonia stuttered. "I must go."

I twisted around to stare at my host, making sure to keep my expression neutral when I explained, "I wanted to offer my condolences and ask what might have happened to her father."

Professor Baccarin raised a surprised eyebrow.

"My esteemed colleague met with a terrible accident, Mrs Fisher. It was in all the papers. You're not suggesting there was something more to it?" he asked in a scoffing tone.

There was something about the people in the museum that just didn't quite sit right with me. Professor Baccarin's student was lying about his past and appeared to have gone to elaborate lengths to support his concocted story. Now another member of the museum staff, the dead professor's daughter no less, appeared to be terrified.

There was going to be a time to find out why. I was not yet ready for that though; I had questions about the coin first.

Sonia Noriega and the San José

S onia's arrival had served as a calming period, allowing Professor Baccarin to return to a more academic state.

Now that we were seated once more, he repeated his previous question.

"Mrs Fisher I must know where you obtained this coin." Except this time he phrased it more as a demand.

That's not a tactic that works on me.

"You first, Professor Baccarin. Why don't you explain its significance?"

Holding up the coin so we could all see it, the professor said, "This is a Felipe VI Segovia Spanish Gold Eight Escudos. There are hardly any in existence and I can tell from the minting year that this coin was one carried on a fabled ship which sank in 1708. It is of enormous historical importance. Please, tell me where you obtained it.”

I considered his request for a moment and chose not to answer. Not yet.

Recalling the name Barbie gave me, I asked, “You mentioned the name 'San José' that is the ship to which you refer?”

“Yes, it is.”

I made an educated guess that if I am honest wasn't much of a stretch given what I already knew.

“It was a treasure ship, wasn't it?”

Professor Baccarin's cheeks coloured slightly. “Well, yes, but that's not what makes it so historically important. The real treasure is in the artefacts we will find on board. I must know where it sank.” He was all but pleading with me.

“I'm afraid I do not have that information, professor.” He was going to challenge me, so I ploughed onward. “The coin was in the possession of a man found murdered below decks on the Aurelia, the cruise ship on which I work and reside. My interest in the coin extends only to my desire to solve his murder since it happened in my jurisdiction.”

I got a nudge from Sam. He had his phone out and on the screen was a report on the San José. One line in bold type jumped off the page –

the cargo in the San José's hold was estimated to be worth more than ten billion US dollars in today's market.

In the last few minutes I had learned the name of the shipwreck the fake Professor Noriega mentioned, and the reason for his interest in it. Billions. Many would deem the figure worth killing for.

Changing tack slightly, I said, "I wish I could tell you more, Professor, but I am not able to provide you with information regarding the victim at this time. However, I hope that we might continue to communicate on this matter when I leave here." I wanted his full cooperation and baited the carrot deliberately. "Purple Star Cruise Lines will surrender all the coins ..."

"All the coins?"

Ooops.

"There are more?"

I couldn't easily deny it now. "Lots, Professor. Plus gemstones, cut and uncut. The victim had several uncut gems in his abdomen. They were found during autopsy. The treasure does not interest me, Professor. That a man would attempt to access it posing as Professor Noriega several days after his death does."

I gave my statement a second to sink in.

Professor Baccarin's brow creased in confusion.

"I'm sorry. I don't follow. You are saying someone ... what? Dressed up as Julio and tried to get the coins?"

"Actually, only a few people close to me and now you know about the coins, Professor. The man we met claimed to be Professor Noriega and he was reacting to a leaked story about the uncut gems. Quite how he knew that connected to the San José, I cannot speculate, but he mentioned a shipwreck. It was one of the first things he did say."

"Who was he?"

I choked on a laugh. "If I knew that, Professor, we would not be talking. Whoever he is, he chose to impersonate your recently deceased colleague. Why would he do that?"

Professor Baccarin's eyebrows climbed his head before he said, "Because Julio Noriega is … was the world's leading authority on the San José." He pushed back with his feet on the carpet, wheeling his chair to the wall where he used his left hand to point to the photographs of the diving expedition. "This is the closest he ever got. Which is to say he allowed himself to be fooled into thinking he might have found it. The wreck divers discovered off the coast of Peru in 1993 was in the right place according to the evidence he was able to amass and the first few pieces of hull we salvaged were the right design for the era. It was when we found the cannons that our hopes were dashed."

Sam asked, "What about the cannons?"

Professor Baccarin explained that the cannons fitted to the San José were more ornate in design than most ships in the merchant fleet. Adorned with dolphins, the salvage team knew they had found a different ship the instant the first cannon was uncovered on the seabed.

"History does not give up its secrets so easily," he lamented.

It was fascinating, but it told me nothing about Finn Murphy or why he came to be stabbed to death in the bowels of the Aurelia. Nor did it tell me anything about the man who threatened to kill me and Barbie just a couple of days ago. Whoever he was, he had gone to a good deal of trouble and expense to find me, and he knew about Finn Murphy, a detail that wasn't in the report Angelica unhelpfully leaked.

The mystery man knew more than me, which wasn't difficult at this stage, but it did bother me. I was behind and that was unacceptable.

Focussing on that, I asked, "Have you ever heard the name Finn Murphy?" I watched the professor's face to see if there was a flicker of recognition.

I saw nothing, and he said, "No. Is the name important?"

I wasn't about to reveal the name was that of the murder victim who had the coins and jewels in his possession.

"Could it be someone that Professor Noriega knew?"

I got a shrug this time. "That I cannot say."

Barbie asked, "Would it be possible to see recent electronic communications Professor Noriega received? He might have messages that reveal what was happening in the days leading up to his death?"

Professor Baccarin's head swung in her direction, a questioning look forming as he read between the lines.

I chose to fill in the blank and remove any ambiguity.

"It is very possible the man we met murdered Professor Noriega prior to assuming his identity."

Professor Baccarin scoffed, "Surely you must be joking. My colleague's death was an untimely accident. Nothing more."

"And his assistant?" Barbie pressed. "He died mere hours before his boss. You think that a coincidence?"

Before the professor could respond, I did my best to smooth the path.

"If someone knew the location of the San José, what might that information be worth?" It was a rhetorical question, and I did not wait for an answer. "And who might they seek out to corroborate what they believed they had found?" Again, I gave my question a second to sink in. "There is a trail of bodies, Professor, and they lead to the San José. I believe it has been found and the man we met is killing his way to the location. He doesn't know where it is yet, but that might be just a matter of time."

My serious line delivered, the room fell silent.

Until a shot rang out the very next moment, startling my heart into skipping a beat.

Crime Scene

N o one moved. A second ticked by as we all looked at each other. Then, as if an electric shock had been fired into our collective backsides, we were all moving at once.

There was no questioning what we heard – it was a single shot fired from a low-calibre handgun. It worries me that I have heard so many shots being fired in recent times that I can tell one type of weapon from another.

I started for the door, taking a step before my brain stopped me. Reversing direction in a hurry, I snatched the gold coin from Professor Baccarin's hand, mouthed an apology, and started running.

Barbie spun her wheels, whipping her wheelchair out and around and in so doing got in everyone's way. Almost running over Jermaine's toes as he fought to get to the door, he chose to jump aside so she could pass. The moment she did, he grabbed the handles and started shoving.

She wailed, "Whoa!" as she turned left on two wheels outside the professor's office door.

Jermaine didn't slow down though and had both me and Sam hot on his heels.

Hanging out of his door and looking startled and perplexed, Professor Baccarin cried, "Where are you going? That sounded like a gun being fired!"

I didn't have the breath to answer and doubted I could explain why we were running toward the sound. Or rather, not the sound itself, but the scream that came after. It hadn't followed instantly like it might if the person was witness to the shot being fired. Nor was it the sound of someone screaming in pain because they had been shot.

Much like my ability to tell weapon calibres apart, it pained me that I knew one type of scream from another. This one came from a young woman and was that of horrific distress. It lasted for several seconds and when it died away was replaced by the keening sound of the same woman as she came to grips with the awful sight she had to be seeing.

Running toward gunfire might sound like a silly thing to do, and I guess I wouldn't argue if you chose to make that point. However, I came here to solve a murder and since walking through the doors of the museum a little more than half an hour ago, I had seen a stack of different clues to suggest something was going on.

There were more shouts ahead – other people reacting – and we almost collided with two men in security guard uniforms as we careened into another corridor.

Right at the back of the museum now, among the libraries and artefact rooms set aside for storing the many, many antiquities it housed, the woman's voice had gone quiet, and we were forced to slow our pace as we searched for her location.

The security guards were going door to door, shoving each one roughly open to peer inside before moving on.

Which of the many doors I could see was the one we wanted?

I got my answer a scant second later when one opened.

The person behind it was moving with stealth; swinging the door quietly lest it make a noise, then peering around the edge of the doorframe, checking the opposite direction first before turning their head to look our way.

Sonia Noriega's eyes widened the instant she saw us all looking back at her, and a curse dropped from her lips as she took off running.

The security guards, bellowed for her to stop and gave chase. However, armed only with whistles – an ineffective deterrent in my opinion – she paid them no mind and was out of sight around a corner almost before I could get my feet moving.

Running after her with Sam, Jermaine, and Barbie ahead of me, I shouted … correction, I wheezed between laboured breaths for them to stop just as we were getting to the room Sonia had exited.

It didn't take long to see what had made Sonia scream.

A pair of feet wearing men's black loafers poked from behind a table. The rest of the body was obscured by wooden boxes which were both on the table and stacked on the floor around it. Idly observing that they might more accurately be called packing crates, I made my way across the room, holding my breath and willing myself to do what I knew was necessary.

I heard a gunshot and I saw a woman running from the scene. Add that to the 'very' still body lying mostly out of sight, and I fully expected to find there was nothing I could do for the victim. However, I had to check.

Drawing level with the end of the table and being careful not to disturb his feet, I forced my head and eyes to look down.

"Patty?" asked Barbie, the question she was asking not needing to be voiced.

I shook my head and looked away.

I suppose technically I ought to have checked for a pulse, but the bullet had been aimed at the person's head and there was no question in my mind that he was beyond saving. I looked away as swiftly as I could, but there were conclusions to draw from the image now indelibly etched into my brain.

The first was the handgun. It was in the victim's hand, his index finger snug against the trigger with the rest of his digits wrapped around the grip. That I was looking at a suicide was obvious. Very obvious.

Too obvious?

Let's put a pin in that one for now and come back to it.

The weapon was an automatic handgun, a squat, black thing I could not identify just by looking. I took a picture of it.

Breaking my train of thought, Jermaine voiced one of the thoughts banging about inside my head, "Madam, that was Professor Noriega's daughter you saw fleeing the scene."

There were more people coming now, the sound of their running feet disturbing the near silence of the museum as they hurried to arrive. They didn't know where they were going though, or so it seemed for they were yelling at each other and into their radios.

With a nod at Sam, I said, "Close the door."

He did so without questioning me and before Barbie could ask, I said, "We have until they arrive to toss this room. Professor Noriega was murdered, I'm almost certain of it. So was his research assistant and now we find his daughter mixed up in something. Somehow, this all leads back to Finn Murphy and the treasure. I have no idea what is going on," I confessed as I used a tissue to open a drawer in the table by the body, "but if there are clues here, we have only seconds to find them."

There was no need for conversation; we all knew the drill and had poked around enough crime scenes now to know how to do so efficiently.

Jermaine gave Barbie a hand to get out of her wheelchair. Her left ankle was bound and supposed to remain out of use, but taking a few stuttering steps wouldn't set her recovery back too far, I hoped.

On the table, I found paperwork. All in Portuguese, I couldn't read it, but hastily snapped pictures that would allow for later scrutiny.

The crates on the floor were sealed, the lids hammered into place. On the table were two open crates. One was empty and the one next to it was full to the brim with those polystyrene peanut thingies.

Grimacing at the door – I could hear the people outside coming closer, I dug a hand into the peanuts and rummaged until I found what was inside: an inelegant jug with a crack running down one side and a chip missing out of the top edge. If pushed to guess, I would say it was a thousand years old or more. I placed it back into the crate.

On the desk to my left, bubble wrap had been opened to reveal a fossil. Much like those I'd seen in Professor Geller's office, it was dark brown and rough. It had been in the bubble wrap, but wasn't now. I picked it up. I will admit I couldn't tell an Iguanodon from an Ichthyosaur but would bet money the thing I had in my hand was the tooth of a dinosaur.

The bubble wrap had been cut open recently; a pair of scissors lay on the table next to it. I put the fossilised tooth back down and moved on.

To my side and kneeling over the body to carefully pat down his clothing, Jermaine had to move away from the growing pool of red liquid.

"Madam," he warned, pointing out that I too was about to find my shoes overrun. Now that I was looking his way, he showed me the man's ID. Hector Benzali wore a lanyard around his neck with his name and picture on it. He worked at the museum, but it did not say what he did.

The voices outside were even closer now, the people – whoever they were – going door to door, guided by the distinctive sound of voices coming over their radios. I guessed it was more members of the museum's security detachment.

This assumption proved accurate a moment later when the door to the room swung open and a face popped into view. By then we had moved away from the body and assumed a relaxed and hopefully innocent-looking posture.

The security guard, her hat on a little skewwhiff, was already backing out again when her brain caught up with her eyes. She performed a classic double take, her surprise at seeing the four of us delaying her response by only a fraction of a second.

Barbie gave the woman a pinky wave as she yelled for her colleagues to join her.

They burst into the room and just as we had, they spotted the body instantly. Yelling in Portuguese for us to stay still and back toward the window, the second guard through the door, a young man with a shaped beard, chose to check the body for signs of life.

Rather thoroughly, in fact, and I found myself yelling at him when he tried to turn the body over.

The guards – there were four of them – had split their attention between us and the body. The two facing my friends and me had no weapons, but had fanned out to block our exit. The woman was talking rapid-fire into her radio until I shouted for her companion to stop what he was doing.

Barbie explained as quickly as she could, warning them not to disturb the crime scene without me needing to express it in English first.

It turned out the woman was in charge, and I was thankful to see the men complied when she turned Barbie's advice into a command.

The police were coming, as one might expect and, of course, we were going nowhere. Found at the scene of an apparent suicide victim, the security guards were right to insist we remained in their custody.

Not that they tried to restrain us. We were escorted from the room and into the hallway outside where we waited, sandwiched between the guards for more than twenty minutes.

Barbie complained that her butt was going dead from all the sitting and was allowed to get up and move about with Jermaine helping her.

The security team didn't recognise my face or my name and when they asked why we were in the room with the body, I explained that we heard the shot and scream and chose to see if there was anything we could do.

They didn't believe me, but they also didn't bother to challenge what I told them.

The cops arrived, their pace unhurried for they were not trying to prevent loss of life and had been told what to expect.

Wouldn't you know it though? The man despatched to manage the investigation was the one cop in the city I had hoped to never see again.

A New Nemesis?

Captain Santoro was talking to a subordinate when he came into view. Maybe he heard my exasperated sigh and maybe his gaze just happened to look in my direction at the same time. Either way, he twitched when he saw who he was looking at and I got to watch as his face turned to thunder.

Was that better or worse than if he had grinned like a cat with the cream?

Approaching our little group, he said, "I believe you will find that we are very much inside *my* jurisdiction now, Mrs Fisher." He tilted his head, aiming an ear in my direction to encourage a response. "No? Nothing to say? What a pleasant relief."

Dismissing me with his next breath, he switched to Portuguese, grilling the museum's security team, and leaving us in the corridor while he was taken to see the body.

When an hour later, he finally ran out of reasons not to talk to us, Captain Santoro had at least seen through the staged suicide.

"You are free to go," he announced handing me a business card with his name and contact details on it. "If you recall anything that you believe will be of use in *my* investigation, please call that number."

I blinked. "Wait, what? Just like that?"

The captain was already turning away when I spoke, and had to reverse his direction to reply.

"You wish to confess to the murder?"

Barbie blurted, "WHAT?" instantly defensive.

I calmed her with a hand on her shoulder.

Captain Santoro stood so he was facing me and came close enough that I could smell his cologne. Crossing his arms over his chest, he looked down at me.

"Mrs Fisher you are a famous busybody. I assume that is why you thought it acceptable to invade a crime scene and poke around. That is what you were doing, yes?"

Truly, I wanted to counter his attitude with one of my own, perhaps challenge him to see what he had noticed in the room with the body, but he was offering us a chance to escape and the only sensible thing I could do was grasp it.

Sullenly, I said, "Yes."

I got a nod of acknowledgment from him.

"I have a murder staged to look like a suicide. Any fool could see the gun could not have stayed in his hand and gripped the way it was and there is no gunshot residue on the victim's hand. It is a shoddy attempt by Miss Noriega to cover up the murder of her boyfriend."

Barbie echoed, "Her boyfriend?"

Captain Santoro's overdue and expected smug grin emerged.

"Yes. This is called police work. My team have already established that Miss Noriega has been heard arguing with her boyfriend at volume in recent days. What we are witness to is most likely a lover's tiff gone too far and will prove to be the result of a third party introduced as a new lover. I have seen this a thousand times. The people of Rio are passionate, Mrs Fisher. Passionate and fiery. This couple, they flew too close to the sun and … well, you have seen the result. Sonia Noriega will not avoid custody for very long. An open and shut case, as you like to say in England, no?"

I dipped my head, a gesture of congratulations.

"Well done, Captain Santoro. You said we could go?"

His eyes narrowed for a moment and his lips parted when a word began to form. He changed his mind though, the thoughts swirling in his head making him cautious.

Biting on his bottom lip, he unfolded his arms and brought up a finger that he wagged in the air with a knowing smile.

"Very good, Mrs Fisher. You wish to make me think you will play ball, that is the expression, yes? But the moment you are out of my sight, you will begin to poke around again. Am I wrong?"

"Not wrong at all," beamed Sam, answering for me and doing so with his usual absolute honesty.

I wanted to bonk him on the head with something.

Unwilling to lie directly to the captain's face, I tried instead to reason with him.

"There is something bigger going on here than a lover's quarrel ending badly. Sonia's father was murdered just a week ago ..."

Captain Santoro held up a hand to stop me.

"Professor Julio Noriega was killed in an automobile hit and run, Mrs Fisher. There are dozens of these unfortunate incidents every year. There is nothing about the circumstances of her father's death that can be considered suspicious."

"Oh, come on!" I exclaimed. "The professor's research assistant was killed only hours earlier! Do you think he was accidentally stabbed to death? That's three deaths in little over a week, all from not only the same museum but all connected. If Sonia killed her boyfriend, which I very much doubt, she did so for a reason that has to be investigated."

Captain Santoro's face did nothing for the next two seconds and I wondered what was happening until a raucous laugh burst from his lips.

"Oh, goodness." He slapped his thigh. "No wonder you keep making it into the papers, Mrs Fisher." The laughter shut off like a switch being flicked and he was suddenly in my face. His hands came up by my face and I thought for a moment he was going to grab me.

Jermaine tensed so completely I swear I could feel his body vibrating.

"Let this be fair warning, Mrs Fisher. For the sake of public relations I am letting you go. My chief seems to think arresting you unless I have a cast iron reason to do so will cast a shadow over the department and gain the mayor's disapproval. He is probably correct. Nevertheless, if I catch you anywhere near Sonia Noriega or this investigation, I will not hesitate to slap the cuffs on you myself."

He held my gaze, his eyes boring into mine. He wanted me to challenge him. The incident at the docks had embarrassed him and he wanted payback.

"Can we go now?" I demanded, refusing to let my voice tremble.

I got a flick of his head in answer; a simple gesture – get out.

Follow that Car!

- -

"Why didn't you tell him about the treasure, Patty?" Barbie hissed at me once we were out of the captain's sight. "That's got to be the thing that links the deaths. Hasn't it?"

I waited until we were out in the street before I gave my response. Two of the security guards had escorted us back down through the museum flanked by a pair of cops and I wanted to be sure we were well away from anyone who might hear us.

"Because I believe telling people puts their lives in danger."

We came to a stop to gather ourselves, my three friends all looking at me expectantly.

"Billions. That's the estimated value of the treasure. If we assume Finn Murphy found the location of the San José, and that it cost his life, then we can also assume whoever killed him will willingly kill again to protect what they know."

Barbie asked, "You think it's the crazy guy who tried to kill us in the ladies' restroom on the British Union Isles?"

I shook my head. "No, he wanted us to tell him what we knew about Finn Murphy. I don't think he was behind his death at all."

Sam raised his hand. "Doesn't that mean there are lots of people that know about it then?"

"Not lots necessarily. Certainly two. When we saw Sonia earlier, she looked worried or scared. I couldn't decide which it was at the time and now I think it was probably both. According to Professor Baccarin, her father was the world's leading authority on the San José. We can assume that means he spent years of this life trying to figure out where it sank and following every little clue or breadcrumb left by anyone. It sank or vanished – whichever it is – more than three hundred years ago, so the stories that might have been told or recorded in someone's journal somewhere have been lost to time or twisted by three centuries of Chinese whispers. A further assumption is that his daughter must know vastly more about the subject than the average person. She will have grown up listening to him talk about it."

"So is she now the target?" asked Jermaine.

I could only shrug my shoulders.

"Her father and boyfriend are dead and at this point all we really know is how little we know."

Sam held out his hand.

"I found this, Mrs Fisher."

We all stared down as he unfolded his fingers. As my assistant, Sam is great in many ways. He has a permanently buoyant outlook, and a cheeky grin is never far from his face – these help to keep my mood light when we are dealing with dark matters. He also has an uncanny ability to see things from an angle the rest of us would never consider.

However, his cognitive ability is limited by his condition and ... well, truth be told he looks for clues but rarely finds anything helpful to the case in hand. Looking down at the slip of folded paper resting in the palm of his hand, I prepared myself to say something charitable.

Barbie reached forward to take it and I think we were all surprised when he snatched his hand away.

"No, you'll spill it!" Sam chided, using both hands to carefully unfold the paper.

"Spill it?" Barbie repeated, her eyebrows dancing as she looked closer.

Now I was interested. In the street outside the museum no one spoke as my young assistant revealed his find.

Unable to see because Sam's hands were cupped around the slip of paper, Jermaine asked, "What have you got, Sam?"

Lifting his chin to show us his grin, he announced, "Cocaine."

Barbie's face shot up to look at mine, shock registering in her eyes.

"I think that's what it is anyway," Sam added.

In a huddle formed by our four bodies, the likelihood of the gentle breeze disturbing his find was low, and with that in mind, I took hold of his fingers and splayed them so we could all see.

The slip of paper, which when he first revealed it, I guessed would have writing on, was blank. Sam had torn it from a notepad to form a makeshift envelope. Cradled inside, tiny specs of white powder shifted with the movements of Sam's hand.

I've never seen cocaine before, not in real life. Was that what Sam had found?

"Can either of you confirm that's cocaine?" I aimed my question at Barbie and Jermaine.

Barbie shot me a lopsided expression, "Babes, I don't even use paracetamol."

I got the same response from Jermaine.

Barbie asked, "Where was it, Sam?"

"There was a pile of it in a plastic bag in the corner of the room."

I touched it, dabbing it with the tip of a finger. A few grains stuck to it allowing me to rub them between my thumb and forefinger. There was something familiar about it, but was that just my brain fooling me?

I pressed Sam's fingers inward again, folding the paper back around the powder. "Well done, Sam. Let's keep it safe," I suggested, taking it from him to zip inside my handbag. "We can have a proper look at it later." Had he found drugs? If so, what the heck did that mean? It was an unexpected element that threw into question everything I thought I knew about the situation.

Glancing back at the museum as I questioned what next step I could take, my eyes locked on a figure hurrying across the street.

It was Inigo, Professor Baccarin's grad student. Tracking my eyes, Jermaine saw him too which got Barbie and Sam's attention.

Barbie growled, "Ooh, there's Professor Baccarin's creepy assistant. He's got some explaining to do."

I took a hesitant step forward, my feet twitching while I watched him cross the road. He had to dart between traffic, and I wondered where he might be going in such a hurry. It was the middle of the afternoon which made it too early to be finishing for the day and lunch was unlikely unless his boss had kept him working.

We didn't need long to figure out where he was heading though. Crossing to get to the same side that we were on, Inigo Montoya ducked directly into the back of a waiting car. There was no pause to speak to or greet the driver, and he wasn't being collected by a girlfriend because he would have got in the front were that the case.

Jolted into motion, I snapped my head around to look for a cab only to find Barbie on her feet and waving to the passing cars.

I'll give her this: no one stops traffic like she can. Six cars slammed their brakes on as she hopped on her good leg to make her chest … shall we say 'move dynamically'? Bouncing breasts beneath a radiant smile was all it took to almost cause a crash as the cars behind were forced to swerve and stop.

Picking the nearest car, Barbie opened the passenger door before the driver could realise what was happening.

"Hey, babes!" she purred. "My friends and I need a lift. Would you be an angel and help a girl out?"

Jermaine held the back door for me until I used both hands to shove him through it.

"Get in, Sweetie! Do butlering later." Sam piled in behind me as Barbie curled her pert bottom into the front seat and trailed a lazy finger up the driver's arm.

"Could you follow that car?" she asked with a nod of her head, her voice nothing less than a sensual whisper.

The man in the driver's seat was in his mid-twenties and if I could read his expression correctly was ready to drive straight to church and marry the blonde vision now batting her eyes in his face. Okay, maybe church is a little hopeful on my part. From my angle his trousers looked rather tight in one particular spot, so perhaps a seedy motel somewhere was more what he had in mind.

Whichever it was, he floored the gas, and the car took off like a gazelle with a cheetah on its tail.

Barbie aimed her eyes down the street and pointed.

"That one, babes! The black Mercedes sedan."

He said something to Barbie in Portuguese, his eyes dark and hungry and not at all on the road ahead.

She reached up to gently cup his chin and push his head back the way it ought to be facing.

"Later, babes," she murmured softly. "If you prove yourself worthy, that is. Now don't get too close and don't lose sight of them either."

I caught the driver's eyes when he flicked them up to look in the rear-view mirror and looked away. Catching a lift like this was not the way I wanted to follow Inigo, but Barbie was right that he had some explaining to do. The souped-up Subaru Impreza we found ourselves in was highly conspicuous, not least because it was lime green, but I doubted the driver of the black Mercedes would give it a second look.

With Barbie's guidance, Enrique – it didn't take him long to make sure Barbie knew his name – tailed Inigo admirably. Enrique was only too eager to please of course, although he began to question where we were going once we left the main highways and came into an area that could only be described as dangerous.

"He wants to know where we are going," Barbie translated Enrique's question.

"Don't we all," I remarked, staring at the taillights fifty yards down the street.

The black Mercedes turned left without indicating, and when we got to the same junction, it was nowhere in sight.

Enrique babbled in Portuguese, his words foreign to my ears, but the tone easy to read: nervous. We had led him to a dubious part of the city, and he wasn't comfortable being here despite the busty blonde acting like she was a sure thing.

He cruised along the street, going slow at Barbie's request. There were cars parked on both sides of the narrow backstreet that was a mix of run down housing and low rent businesses. Half a dozen roller doors provided potential hiding places for the black sedan, but we were never going to find it if we stayed in the car.

Twisting around to look at he back seat, Barbie asked, "What do you think?"

It was decision time. The sensible option was to ask Enrique to take us back to the museum. I would hand him a worthy tip for helping us. A far cry from what he hoped to get from Barbie, I'm quite certain, but if we did that, there was no chance to find out where Inigo had gone or who he was with.

My itchy skull insisted he was up to something secret and shady. He lied about his time at U of C, was in direct contact with Sonia Noriega only minutes before her boyfriend was killed and Sam had very possibly found drugs.

Making the only decision I could, I gritted my teeth and said, "We go on foot."

How to Solve a Problem like Patricia

X avier Silvestre tapped Gomez on the shoulder.

"Stop here." They had just driven past the junction the lime green Subaru turned into. It was stopped halfway down the street and the people inside were getting out.

Quite what they were doing or why they chose to follow the black Mercedes, Silvestre had no idea. Clearly Patricia Fisher was playing the role of detective again. He'd heard the shot earlier and saw the police arrive.

Dressed as an elderly janitor, he was in the museum's staff reception when Patricia Fisher arrived. She passed within touching distance of him without once looking his way. He knew from experience carrying a mop and bucket around allowed him to go wherever he pleased, and he did just that without a single member of museum staff questioning who he was. The only time he felt a need to duck out of the way was when more cleaning staff appeared in a hallway ahead of him.

There had been a shooting; that much was easy to gather. Quite why Mrs Fisher chose to involve herself was curious, but equally Silvestre didn't have enough interest to care what the answer might be.

He wanted to get Patricia Fisher alone and her decision to head into Rio's slummier favelas played right into his hands. He had contacts here already. All he needed to do now was activate them.

Gomez could take care of the butler; the one member of Mrs Fisher's group Silvestre knew to be capable. However, he wanted to keep his valet in reserve for when the time was right. Unlike Silvestre, who could don a false nose, a hairpiece, and a change of clothing to instantly transform into someone new, Gomez was most of seven feet tall. It didn't matter what disguise he wore, people would remember him.

"I follow?" Gomez asked, typically keeping his sentence brief.

Silvestre grabbed his door handle. "No. Pull up along the road." The phone in the murderous treasure hunter's hand connected. "One moment," he requested of the voice at the other end. To Gomez he said, "I must track their movements until our 'friends' arrive. They will take care of the necessary unpleasantness. Be ready for my return. I shall be bringing Mrs Fisher with me."

Gomez nodded his head to acknowledge the instructions, but his boss was already halfway out of the car. Talking into the phone, he walked away without glancing back.

Backstreet Secrets

- -

"**M**adam, I recommend we remain here as briefly as possible." Jermaine's voice was firm when he made the request. Curtains had twitched when we exited the car, but it was Enrique's decision to hurtle back toward a safer postcode that had me on edge.

Barbie pouted at his speedily departing taillights as if she had been dumped or turned down somehow.

I grabbed her arm. "Don't worry. We still have to get back yet. You can go fishing for lifts again shortly."

On the other side of the street, Sam was already listening at a roller door.

"There are voices inside," he whispered just barely loud enough for us to hear.

I started tiptoeing across the street, stopping after just a couple of paces when I realised what was missing.

"Where's your wheelchair?" I gasped, staring down at Barbie's bandaged leg.

She hobbled by me with a shrug.

"There wasn't time. It will either be there when we get back, still sitting at the side of the road outside the museum, or it won't be."

"I think the latter is more likely."

I got another shrug. "Too late now."

Pushing it to one side, I hurried after her, joining Sam and Jermaine as they listened at the roller door.

There was a faded and peeling sign painted on the roller door to advertise a firm that specialised in repairing air conditioning systems if I was reading it correctly. It wasn't even four o'clock and the place showed no signs of operating as a business, so I had to guess their enterprise had failed at some point in the past.

There were other businesses in the street and not one of them looked to be open. Sam had left us to explore some of the other roller doors, listening at each one before moving on.

"Can you understand what they are saying?" I asked, my voice as quiet as I could make it.

Barbie scrunched up her face; doing all she could to improve her hearing. Like me though, she could hear the conversation inside, but not the words being said.

"We need to find a window or something," I muttered, stepping away from the roller door.

Jermaine's arm blocked my path.

"Madam, please allow me. This situation feels risky, even against the usual backdrop of drama that surrounds us."

I believe he employed 'us' when really he meant 'me'. The drama in our lives doesn't gravitate toward anyone other than me. It can be a little trying at times.

Stepping to the side, Jermaine peered around the side of the building.

"There is a window, madam," he reported, leaving us behind as he set off. I hurried after him leaving Barbie to keep an eye on Sam.

There was indeed a window. It was next to a door and was set with frosted glass. A corner of the glass was missing though, the damage ignored for however long it had been that way. It didn't even look as though anyone had tried to cover it with a piece of tape.

The two of us peered through the small hole, our faces almost pressed together so we could both see inside.

A person blocked our view, the man's back filling the field of vision. He moved, saying something I didn't catch, and revealing what lay beyond. My jaw dropped open.

We were looking into the space behind the roller door; an open void one might expect to see filled with work benches and people working on air conditioning units if the business advertised was in operation. Instead, there were two long benches set up with monitors and computers. I couldn't see what was on the screens, the angle was wrong, but I saw Inigo walk by and that confirmed we had the right place.

More than that, it confirmed I had been right to suspect him. I counted five people – four men and a woman. The men were all in their thirties or forties with the exception of Inigo and the woman was maybe late twenties.

Tall and lean, her dark hair was pulled into a short ponytail.

On the floor to the left of the tables, a waste bin overflowed with takeaway cartons and fast-food wrappers.

Inigo was explaining something to the woman and two of the men. The remaining man sat in front of a monitor. Whatever Inigo had to say, he was gesticulating wildly, getting emotional about the subject matter. Was he talking about me? Was this something to do with the treasure?

Jermaine whispered, "Madam, we should go."

I didn't argue, relieved to have found something to confirm my suspicions about Professor Baccarin's grad student, and aware there was nothing to be gained from hanging around here any longer.

Sam returned just as Jermaine and I stepped back into the street. "I can't hear anything at the other doors, Mrs Fisher," he reported dutifully.

Behind him, all the way down at the corner of the street, movement caught my eye as a lone figure stepped out of a shadow and then back into it. There was no time to see who it was, and though I didn't recognise the outline I saw, there was something familiar about it all the same. However, it was the furtive nature of the person's movements that made the hair on the back of my neck stand on end.

I grabbed Sam's hand.

"I think we ought to be going."

Jermaine heard the timbre of my voice, reacting to it by spinning in a slow arc to look for danger.

"Patty?" questioned Barbie, her own voice betraying the nerves she felt.

"Yes, time to go," I decided. Inigo was up to something shady. Probably something illegal. To solve the murder of Finn Murphy, or at least figure out how the museum and the events there were connected, I needed to figure out what it was. It would have to wait though because every nerve in my body screamed that we were in danger.

There was no sign of the figure I'd seen now. If he was still there watching us, he was making good use of the shadows. It was time to leave.

"Barbie, can you get an Uber or something?" I asked, angling away from the figure I'd seen and starting to walk down the street.

Her phone was in her hand a heartbeat later.

"I can try."

She didn't even get time to open the App before a double cab utility truck roared into view at the end of the road. It had bright lights fitted above the cab and more set into the grill. They made my eyes hurt to look at. Coming our way, the streetlights silhouetted two men standing in the back load bed. One slapped a hand on top of the truck's roof to make a distinctive donging sound.

The truck drew to a halt and the doors opened.

"Patty, I can't run," squeaked Barbie. It was the opposite of our usual problem which was more a case of me not being able to keep up.

"Madam, I suspect these gentlemen have hostile intentions," Jermaine remarked in his usual understated manner. "Might I, on this occasion, employ an early offense as a tactic?"

The men in the load bed had jumped down to the street, flexing their knees as they bounced back to upright. Joining their friends as they left the cab, all four came our way.

I bit my lip. "Sweetie, I don't like that idea. What if they just want to ask directions?" I hated that Jermaine had to fight sometimes. Ok, so he is really good at it and uses his legs and arms like they are a lawn mower, but even the best fighter gets hurt and he was no exception.

"Give us everything you have!" barked the man who had been in the truck's passenger seat. "Consider it a Rio tax."

Jermaine jinked a single eyebrow at me in question.

I sighed. "Oh, all right then."

Xavier Silvestre expected to see the four local thugs kill Patricia Fisher's friends and grab her before any of them could figure out what was happening. The problem, he lamented as he watched the Jamaican bodyguard run, leap, and fell the first man with a superman punch, was that outsourced thugs always felt a need to get inventive.

He wanted a simple job. There was no need for any of them to say anything. Kill the older woman's companions and remove from their bodies any wallets or loose items they might be holding. Xavier Silvestre knew Mrs Fisher had the gems found inside Finn Murphy's gut and assumed she would have taken at least one of them with her to the museum.

Clearly, the goons he believed he could trust had read between the lines, concluding there was something of value to be found.

Cocking his pistol, he watched.

Jermaine's first strike shunted the target's chin back more than a yard and ensured he wasn't getting up any time soon. Landing in a crouch, he pirouetted on his palms like a gymnast, swinging his legs up and around to sweep the feet of two more men.

Sam and Barbie, despite their limitations, were running to lend their weight to the fight and I knew I had to do the same.

My heart hammered in my chest, imploring me to run away and it was only fear for my friends that drove me to join in.

The one remaining man on his feet yanked a gun from his trousers. It was coming up and around, lining up with Jermaine's back as he delivered a hammer blow to knock out a second of the attackers.

I swung my handbag – I know, what a cliché – but what else was I going to do? Punch him in the face? I would have broken my hand. Just before he could pull the trigger, my handbag smacked into his forearm, driving his aim upward.

A shot fired into the air, followed instantly by the sound of a window smashing and a scream coming from within the house it belonged to.

Sam barrelled into the gunman, wrapping his arms around him as he drove him back. It wasn't enough. Sam weighs more than me but he isn't exactly heavy. The energy of his assault was quickly absorbed and then converted.

Planting his feet, the man gripped Sam around the shoulders, swinging him off the ground and letting go. Sam crunched into a car and all I could do was watch with horror as the gun lined up on him.

There was an unexpected roar of engine; enough to make the man with the gun twist to look. He did so in time to see Barbie behind the wheel of the utility vehicle before the front end slammed into his chest.

The blow blasted him backward with a muffled cry of pain. Sam had to roll out of the way as the man crashed into the bonnet of the same car he'd come to rest on and we all got to watch the gunman's head crack the windshield from the force of his impact.

Speechless, I stood staring.

The gun clattered back to earth, jolting me into motion just as Barbie screamed, "Get in!"

A curse in Portuguese ended abruptly when Jermaine kicked out a foot. He'd taken out three of the attackers all by himself, rendering two unconscious and now a third as the only one still fighting slumped to the ground.

Snatching at Sam, I snagged the sleeve of his shirt and dragged him with me.

Barbie was at the wheel of the attackers' car. We were stealing it, but I doubted they were about to report that fact to the police. As if hearing my thoughts, a siren sounded in the distance – the homeowner with the shot-out window no doubt feeling the need to make a call.

Stepping out of his shadowy hiding place once more, Xavier Silvestre could not believe his eyes. The bungling morons had botched the job completely. Handed the element of surprise, they had squandered it all and now lay motionless in the street.

Before his eyes, Patricia Fisher was bundling her handicapped assistant into the truck. The butler was diving in the other side, and he had about two seconds to change the outcome.

Raising his handgun, Silvestre aimed at the English woman. Not a kill shot; that wouldn't do. What he needed was to wound her. If he did that before she got into the car, the rest would bail out to get her. Delaying their escape would seal their fate because he would shoot each of them in rapid succession.

Stilling his body, he lined up his shot. Her hip, that would do the trick. No danger of hitting a vital organ and a big enough target to ensure he wouldn't miss.

A gentle squeeze of the trigger ...

Calm and Dignified at all Times.

I was just clambering into the car when a hand snaked out to grab my ankle - one the attackers was still going. I squealed in fright, spasming on the spot and twisting to see where it had come from. In the same instant, I heard a shot and less than a nanosecond after it, something whacked into the car door right by my bottom.

What was I supposed to do with my eyes? Which direction was I supposed to look in?

Barbie's voice filled my head, "Patty! Get in!"

The hand around my ankle gave a yank.

Naturally, I said, "Waaaaaaah!" in a thoroughly calm and British manner as I pitched to the side and swam my arms through the air to grab the car.

Another shot echoed in the street, and this time something tugged at my handbag. I had it looped over my head by the shoulder strap and suddenly it wasn't there anymore, it was falling to the ground.

"I think someone just shot at me!" I managed to gibber, my mouth moving even though I couldn't convince the rest of my body to do anything.

In the second and a half since the first shot, Jermaine had flung himself across the back seat of the car.

I heard him say, "Excuse the manhandling, please, madam," as he gripped my jacket by the lapels and yanked me bodily into the car. I landed on top of Sam, but found myself on the floor a heartbeat later when Barbie stomped on the gas.

Going in reverse at something a little north of warp speed, she had her head down and twisted from the waist to see through the back window. It was a good thing too because three neat bullet holes appeared in the windscreen where her face would have otherwise been.

Whoever the shooter was, they wanted to stop this car and they didn't care who they killed to do it.

My door was still open, but it swung shut when Barbie spun the steering wheel. Leaving the shooter behind, she angled the car through a tight right turn in reverse and just kept going.

A yell of, "Hang on to something!" was the only warning we got before she demonstrated her driving ability by performing a perfect skidding one hundred and eighty degree turn. Now facing the right way, plumes of blue smoke erupted from the tyres as they fought for traction against the amount of torque she was putting through the wheels.

With Jermaine's help, I levered myself off the floor of the truck and into the centre seat between him and Sam.

I got one glimpse of the shooter – it was the vaguely familiar figure I spotted earlier.

"Patty?" Barbie angled her eyes in the rear-view mirror to meet mine. "Who was that?"

Loose Ends

Xavier Silvestre stooped to collect the spent brass from his weapon – it didn't pay to leave the cops any clues. They were coming; their sirens getting closer, but he had a few moments yet. A few moments to tidy up the loose ends.

The team of thugs were all still alive, but they were hurt and the one who got hit by their own vehicle was in need of medical treatment.

Silvestre shot him at point blank range. Three more shots ended the protest coming from his companions, though it required another bullet to be sure the last of them wouldn't be getting quizzed by the police.

Collecting the shell casings as before, he used his phone to have Gomez meet him at the far end of the street – better that way and less likely the police would see his car.

Though he doubted the handbag would contain anything of interest, there was the chance Mrs Fisher might have been carrying an uncut gem in it. Also, her phone could prove useful.

Collecting it from the ground just as Gomez pulled the car to a halt, Silvestre was securely inside and leaving the area when he found the single gold coin. It made his heart skip a beat for he knew precisely what it was and what its presence meant.

The coin changed everything. The stakes increased instantly. A moment ago, he'd believed Finn Murphy had found … something. That it could be the location of the ship's treasure was a very real possibility he refused to let himself truly believe. Now he couldn't deny it.

He'd been right all along. The San José and its crew hadn't gone to a watery grave courtesy of the British. Her captain and officers chose to steal it instead, faking their ship's destruction to ensure no one ever came looking for them.

The gold coins could have been melted down, of course, but the jewellery, the ornate family heirlooms … it was inconceivable that all could be hidden from the world if they had not been shared out among the thieves.

No, something else had befallen the San José, an unexpected fate that kept the treasure hidden for all these years. Except it was no longer hidden. The coin proved it and where there was one, there had to be more.

Slouching into the sumptuous leather of his seat, Silvestre knew what he had to do.

"Gomez, I have a task for you."

Dinner and Research

Shockingly, Barbie's wheelchair was where we left it. In fact, it looked as though someone had carefully wheeled it away from the edge of the pavement and parked it against the museum's outer wall. They had even put the brake on.

Jermaine placed it in the load bed of our stolen utility vehicle which we subsequently dumped half a mile from the port. The sun was almost down, but the temperature was pleasant and our meander along the coast road back to the ship would have been delightful had we not all been looking over our shoulders the whole time.

As you might imagine, our conversation focussed heavily on why the four men in the utility truck attacked us, who they were, and the identity of the mysterious fifth man who chose to shoot at us.

"He was there before they attacked," I explained to my friends.

Barbie asked, "What? Like he was watching or something?"

I could only shrug. "He was in the shadows at the end of the road. I spotted him right before they showed up. Thinking about it now, he must have watched the attack and decided to weigh in himself only when we got the upper hand."

"So he was part of it?" concluded Jermaine.

I nodded my head, mostly to myself. "Maybe, yes. Or maybe he was nothing to do with it."

"Then why start shooting?" Barbie wanted to know.

I had an answer I didn't like, "He was the lookout man for Inigo and whatever he is up to with his friends."

No one had anything to say about that.

Ship's security recognised us approaching long before we got to them, but dutifully requested to see our identification as they ought. I already knew my passport was gone, of course; it was in my handbag. My purse and therefore my credit cards, the priceless gold coin and a dozen other personal items got left in a Rio back street during our escape.

It could all be replaced ... well, not the coin, but that wasn't mine anyway, but the inconvenience of replacing my passport was one I could do without. I wasn't the first passenger ever to suffer this problem, so my return was logged along with the report of my passport being lost and I was welcomed aboard with everyone else.

Calls to the rest of my team, made during our walk through the port, had them hurrying to join us in my suite. I hadn't made the calls, of course, because my phone was in my handbag and presumably gone forever.

Barbie's boyfriend, Dr Hideki Nakamura, who had remained behind today as the on-call duty physician, was also doubling up as dog sitter for my mother and daughter duo of miniature dachshunds. They responded to our arrival by jumping off the couch and running full pelt for the door while barking the whole time.

I believe they were trying to scare away intruders or possibly alert the humans inside their domicile to the potential threat posed by the newcomers. Unfortunately, they are about as scary as an angry hamster.

I scooped them both as they ran up my shins, tucking one under each arm to carry them back into my suite's central living area.

"Yes, ladies, mummy is home. Did you miss me?" I cooed at them, getting doggy kisses on my chin in return.

Hideki was putting his laptop to one side, balancing it on a pile of serious looking medical books to his right. Rising from the couch – a different one to that which the dogs favoured – he greeted Barbie first.

"Quiet day?" he asked, stooping to kiss her cheek.

Barbie sniggered. "Not exactly. I was with Patty. It's never quiet around Patricia 'Bullet Magnet' Fisher.' She made air quotes around my new middle names.

Hideki straightened, shooting me a quizzical look.

I placed Anna and Georgie on the carpet.

"It's not my fault. I don't arrange for these things to happen. I don't call ahead and ask if someone can arrange a murder."

Hideki swung his gaze back to Barbie.

"There was a murder?"

She chuckled in a sad kind of way. "Isn't there always?"

Upon entering the suite, Jermaine had gone directly to the kitchen where he was preparing high tea. Baker and the others would be joining us shortly – we had new knowledge to share with them. It needed to be discussed, and we would spend the evening exploring the San José. Knowing where the gold coins came from and the mystery surrounding the ship, we had a new starting point for working out what happened to Finn Murphy.

In the search for a suspect, I was already firmly focused on the man who posed as Professor Noriega. Clearly possessing murderous intentions, all I had to do was figure out who he was. I suspected that task might prove a little tricky.

With Barbie filling Hideki in on the events of our day, I went to my bedroom and shut the door. Inside and away from my friends, I gave myself a moment to reflect on my latest near-death experience.

How was it that I so constantly found myself embroiled in other people's murderous pursuits? I was a detective on a cruise ship. I ought to be helping out with kids that have wandered away from their parents, an occasional theft from one of the shops, or perhaps even a lost wallet. Instead, I find bodies everywhere I go and habitually follow that up by discovering the killer.

The rational part of my brain suggested, quite insistently, that I ought to quit my job and live a life of luxury just sunbathing and sipping cocktails. I had a benefactor who would see to it that I had everything I ever wanted. The suite I live in is mine in perpetuity. Well, actually, it belongs to the Maharaja of Zangrabar, but he only bought it so I could stay there.

I knew though, that were I to terminate my employment, I would find myself bored in a heartbeat and be peering over the top of a magazine, spying on those around me as I lazed in the sun.

Exhaling deeply, I checked my makeup, reapplied a little lippy, and went in search of tea.

My team of ship's security officers, led by Lieutenant Commander Martin Baker were just arriving.

"A murder?" I heard him say.

Molly's voice echoed in from outside in the corridor as she filed in behind Lieutenant Schneider. "Did someone say murder? Another one?"

Barbie grinned. "Yup. And we all got shot at."

"Again?" questioned Lieutenant Deepa Bhukari, Martin's wife.

Frowning, I found myself getting defensive. "All right, all right. It's not my fault. The murder had nothing to do with me and I have no idea why we got attacked and shot at."

Schneider expressed his confusion, "Wait, are those two separate things? Attacked and shot at?

Sam nodded helpfully. "Yes. There were four men with guns, but Jermaine kicked them in the teeth before they could shoot at us. It was someone else who did the shooting."

Martin's eyes flared. "How did you get away?"

"Stole their car," boasted Barbie proudly.

I waved my hands in the air to break up the conversation.

"Look, the murder is connected to the treasure. At least, I think it is. We showed the coin to one of Professor Noriega's colleagues and ten minutes later, the boyfriend of Professor Noriega's daughter got shot. It was made to look like a suicide, but they did a poor job." I remembered the powder Sam found. "Oh, and Sam found what might be cocaine near the body. We photographed some evidence ..."

My voice trailed off and I muttered something unprintable under my breath.

Barbie knew why. "They were both in your handbag."

"That's a problem?" questioned Deepa which prompted a quick explanation about my handbag.

Jermaine announced that tea was ready – when we are on board for it, he likes to serve tea at four o'clock sharp. We were a little adrift today having not returned until just after four, but it was nice to have a routine all the same and he made such wonderful petite fours.

As a group, we crossed the room, taking up positions around the breakfast bar. Jermaine poured tea into fine, white porcelain cups, the kind that come with a saucer and require an extended pinky finger to drink from.

Barbie had Hideki fetch his laptop and with everyone gathered around her, pulled up search results for the San José. Silence fell, not just because we were grazing on the delicious morsels of food Jermaine made for us, but because we were all reading.

The only words spoken in the next couple of minutes came from Barbie when she asked if we were ready for her to scroll down the page.

There was a lot to read. More than we would get through in an evening, so we broke it down into sections. Martin and Deepa were going to look at the history of the ship, the figures associated with it three hundred years ago and the voyages it took. Barbie, Hideki, and

Jermaine delved into modern reports; anything that sounded like people trying to find it, or artefacts that had surfaced over the centuries.

Anders, Molly, and Schneider dug into the battle where it supposedly sunk in 1708 and the myriad theories regarding what else might have happened if it didn't sink as claimed.

I was looking into Professor Noriega and his assistant, Antonio Bardem. The two men dying mere hours apart was disturbing, but it was the location of the assistant's murder that bothered me. Barbie had been able to find Antonio's home address when she initially researched the mysterious Professor Noriega. That was only hours after the man we believed to be the professor tried to stab us in a ladies' toilet.

Antonio lived just a few blocks from the museum, but his body was found all the way across town. There could have been a dozen reasons for him to be where he was, but I wasn't ready to believe any of them. His murder was connected to the treasure, and if he was killed because of it, then so too was Professor Noriega. Okay, so I'd already decided that before my two hours of research, but I felt more firmly convinced now.

Unfortunately, it didn't get me anywhere. What I needed to figure out was why Sonia Noriega's boyfriend had been killed.

Dinner time came around and we broke from our computers to eat.

A knock at my door turned out to be the captain of the ship, Alistair Huntley. Jermaine took the captain's hat, brushing an invisible something from it before placing it carefully on a shelf in the suite's little foyer.

Alistair Huntley is a little bit older than me and is unspeakably handsome. He has no children, no ex-wife, his own money, and he keeps in shape with regular exercise. I'm a little bit in love with him, which is a good thing because he's my boyfriend.

There was a smile on his face when he crossed the room and though he dipped his head in greeting to everyone else, his eyes never left mine for long. I got a kiss on my lips; just a peck because we were with company, and he slid onto the barstool next to mine.

"How's the ship?" I asked.

"The ship," he replied thoughtfully, "is in excellent condition. That is not to say we are without problems to which I must attend. I am, however, finished for the day and hoped you might be free to join me this evening."

That had been our intention, but the nature of our roles often dictates plans must be changed. He was looking around now at the assembled team because it was clear we were deep into something.

"Is this to do with the treasure?" he enquired, reading a few lines from Barbie's open laptop.

Outside of my team, Alistair was the only person in the world who knew about it. I almost kept it from him too, certain in my heart that secrets are best kept by not telling anyone. In the end though, he had a right to know as captain, not least because the fortune in gold and jewels was stored in my suite's safe and had already attracted one murderous madman. Two if we count whoever killed Finn Murphy.

Over dinner, a sumptuous feast of Mexican delicacies, we all exchanged what we had learned. It all boiled down to this: the San José was a Spanish treasure ship, taking gold and precious jewels mined in Peru back to Spain. It left port early, the captain seemingly unwilling to wait for its heavily armed naval escort. Cornered by ships of the British fleet, it sank with all hands when the magazine exploded. That ought to be that, but artefacts known to have been loaded onto the ship had since been found. One in particular bearing a family crest was found in England. Another item was found in Spain. This could not be the case if the ship had sunk as reported.

Martin and Deepa had found a link to an article that could easily be listed as a conspiracy theory. The author suggested a mass grave found in what is now a holiday resort on the western African coast was the final resting place of the San José's crew. Dating of the bodies and the clothes and artefacts found with them aligned with the ship's disappearance. He went on to hypothesise that a portion of the crew, very possibly the officers, had murdered the rest and stolen the ship. They would have been rich beyond any man's wildest dreams, but clearly something had gone wrong with their plan, for the treasure remained hidden to this day.

Except for what I held in my safe.

Finn Murphy had found it. Someone had killed him, and I was willing to bet they did so trying to find out where the enormous horde of gold and jewels were.

I wasn't after the treasure. It wouldn't belong to me even if I was the one who found it. I was just doing my job, solving a murder.

In the morning we were all heading back into Rio and the museum. My chat with Professor Baccarin got cut short earlier and I needed to know more about … everything. Three deaths in a short period of time all linked to the treasure. I couldn't figure out where the cocaine came into it, but Inigo Montoya was involved somehow.

We packed things up, my friends drifting away to their accommodations before it got too late. They took Sam with them, dropping him back at his room – we'd heard from Gloria, and she was already there. Only Alistair remained, kissing me properly once we were alone and tugging my hand to lead me to my bedroom.

Tomorrow. I would get answers about Professor Noriega tomorrow.

Intruder in the Night

I awoke in the night with a need to pee, but I wasn't going to use the toilet in my bedroom. It has no window, or porthole perhaps might be the better word, and turning on the light would have woken Alistair.

Sleepily, and with hurried steps, I tiptoed past the snoring dachshunds in their basket and out into the suite's main living area. The Windsor Suite, built to accommodate royalty, had a selection of places one could go to do the necessary. I chose the nearest which was by the main entrance.

I got three paces before a hand the size of a baseball catcher's mitt closed over my mouth.

My scream, an automatic and instant reaction, never made it past my lips and a second hand, this one attached to a meaty arm, snaked around my waist, pinning both arms to my sides to hold me in place.

Ridiculously, my first thought was a thankful one. Thankful I was wearing a negligee and wasn't naked. That thought was swiftly dismissed by more pertinent ones such as 'Oh, my God, I'm going to die!' and 'Who the heck is the giant currently squeezing the life out of me?'.

The hands held me in place like steel bars, refusing to budge as I thrashed and kicked.

I needed to make a noise; anything to get Alistair's attention. If I could kick over a lamp or a vase of flowers ... it wouldn't take anything more than that. However, my attacker, yes, another one, hauled me from the floor, carting me across the room with his hand still clamped over my mouth.

We were heading for the sun deck, the door to which I expected to find open - otherwise how did he gain entry - but it was locked.

I tried to bite at his fingers, but the hand was clamped so tightly over my mouth, I couldn't open it. I was probably lucky he hadn't covered my nose too or I wouldn't have been able to breathe.

Fighting to get free as I was, I had been carried all the way across the room before I saw what the man had come for - my safe was open. The oil painting it sat behind had been swung wide to give access. Until we put Finn Murphy's haul of gold coins and priceless jewellery inside, the safe had contained only a few of my most precious belongings.

It had never been worth cracking until now, but that's what the man had done. The thick steel door hung open, exposing the emptiness inside. Empty because the contents were in a large black rucksack on the floor beneath.

Squirming, I managed to get an arm free. I raked my nails at the hand over my mouth and might as well have been scratching at a rock for the all the impact I had.

"Stop," the man rasped in my ear, speaking for the first time. His voice had a Spanish accent, I thought, but there was no time to analyse it because we were at the sliding glass door to the sundeck.

I flailed my arm again, slapping it up into his head, hoping I might catch an eye ... anything to make him let go. When I tried to get my bare feet up against the glass, he squeezed with the arm around my waist, crushing me so tightly I saw dancing stars and thought I might pass out.

"Open it," he growled, recognising that to turn the handle himself meant letting go of me.

I shook my head as much as I was able held in his vice grip and continued to fight. If he wanted to go outside, it meant he was going over the side. Or I was. I could survive the fall to the water, and assuming I didn't lose consciousness, would be able to swim to shore. Surely he was coming with me though, tossing me overboard, collecting the gold and following. Whoever he was, I had to find a way to get free.

Twisting his body away from the door, he was forced to put me down so he could open it. I told myself this was my moment – he would have to take an arm off me, and I would be able to use both arms to achieve ... something.

He was savvier than that though. With a flex of his muscles, he flipped my feet into the air, angling me face down and driving me into the carpet. I made a thump when I hit the floor and the air whooshed from my lungs.

Gasping for air when I was already short of breath, any chance I had to get free was taken away. His knee went into the small of my back, pinning me to the carpet as he reached up to unlock the door.

He was incredibly trong and seriously huge. I was yet to see him, but his relative height compared to mine had to make him close to seven feet tall. Terrified, and convinced he would knock me out if I continued to resist, I was beginning to question how cold the water would feel and how long the drop would take when I heard salvation approaching.

The bark of a dachshund is a curious thing. They are so small and cute, one expects to get a yappy little yip from them, but their bark is deep and booming. Not quite that of a Rottweiler or Dobermann perhaps, but far more convincing than their size would suggest.

Anna and Georgie had heard the thump my body made when I hit the carpet. It was enough to make them want to investigate and now the pair of them were racing to get to me and barking all the way.

I heard Alistair shout something, the muffled sound of his voice telling me he was still in bed and confused about what was going on. He'd awoken to the sound of my dogs going crazy.

The giant pinning me to the carpet had managed to unlock the door, but when the dogs arrived, he was finally forced to let me go before he could get it open.

Anna and Georgie will happily go for hours without moving and look about as dangerous as a sock puppet with a sneer, but they can be ferocious when the mood takes them.

In the moonlight, they were little more than dark blurs streaking across the carpet. I didn't need to see them though for they were making all the noise.

The barking stopped when they threw themselves at my assailant, turning to growls and doggy expletives. They wouldn't do much damage, but all I needed was the distraction they caused.

I expected the knee on my back to lift; the man's weight made breathing all but impossible, yet even with my dogs biting him, he didn't move. I felt his arm sweep down and heard Anna squeal when he sent her tumbling.

Fearing for her, I was rewarded with the sound of her snarling once more as she returned to the fight.

Two seconds had passed since they first barked and that was all the time Alistair needed to exit the bedroom. With a bellow that sounded like a melody to my ears, he charged.

The knee pinning me to the carpet lifted; there one moment and gone the next. Alistair's arrival forced the giant to abandon me, so with a huge breath that seemed to inflate my entire chest, I rolled out of the way and shouted for help.

I was halfway through shouting Jermaine's name when he burst from his adjoining cabin. As the butler assigned to the suite, his own accommodation was linked by a door on the far side of the kitchen. It meant he was never far away and boy was I grateful right now.

Scooping the dachshunds, who were both bobbing and weaving to get another bite of the unwelcome intruder, I had to lunge to grab them before someone got stomped on. Scrambling backward on my butt, I hugged the struggling hounds to my chest and tried not to freak out.

The giant swung a fist at my boyfriend's head. It missed as Alistair ducked and he came up with a haymaker of a punch that caught the man on the left side of his jaw.

I wanted it to be one of those Hollywood punches that fells a man in one go. Alas, Alistair was fighting a titan and the blow appeared to have no effect at all. In fact, it was like the man didn't even feel it. His head rocked slightly from the exchange of energy, but that was all.

Jermaine was running across the suite, his lean, muscular body on display save for a pair of silk boxer shorts that were almost doing the job of hiding his necessaries.

With a grunt of exertion and a leap, he angled his body to deliver a kick to the stranger's back. It landed just in time to stop a punch that might have taken Alistair's head off. He'd tried to land another punch only to have it parried and caught. Now the giant had Alistair by his throat and a clubbing fist up high. Only Jermaine's arrival saved him.

Coming to my senses, I picked myself off the carpet and ran for the door.

Behind me, Jermaine was belting seven bells out of the safecracking man mountain, and I knew from experience that my butler would have him subdued in moments. That didn't mean security wasn't required.

Flinging my door open, I screamed for them to come. At that volume and in the dead of night, I was certain my voice would carry all the way to the guard positioned at the elevator leading to the bridge. For that matter, there were always roving patrols around, walking the ship, making sure all is well.

Message delivered, I screamed again for good measure, checking over my shoulder to confirm Jermaine had floored my latest attacker. I almost choked on my shock when I saw the giant still standing.

Jermaine spun, whipping his right leg up and out. He had to jump to get his foot high enough to hit the man's face, but the blow landed. How was it possible that such punishment could be absorbed?

The kick rocked the man back, but when Jermaine followed up with another strike, the giant swung a punch my butler failed to see coming.

I heard the fist connect and was forced to watch with eyes aghast when Jermaine fell backward.

Only hours ago, Jermaine demonstrated his ninja skills by taking on four armed men. Now he was losing to a giant who acted like pain was an incentive to try harder.

Silhouetted by the light coming through the panoramic windows to his rear, the ox of a man stalked forward. Jermaine and Alistair were both down and he was coming for them, coming to finish them off!

I screamed for help again, undoubtedly waking my neighbours, but my desperate demands had been heard and this time I got an answer – a shout of reply.

Ship's security were coming.

And they had guns.

Handbag

I snatched at the light switches, wondering why I hadn't done so before. Nothing happened. I tried again, flicking them down and up. Still nothing.

The safecracker had killed the power and I was darned if I knew how to turn it back on. I don't want to play the helpless woman card, but electricity scares the bejezzus out of me; it would be a desperate day when I opened the fuse box.

Leaning out into the corridor, I saw a pair of guards rounding the corner. They were running close to flat out, one hand holding their hats in place, the other on the butt of their sidearms. The man and woman team spotted me and increased their pace.

"Here! In here! He's trying to kill the captain!" I yelled, running back inside because I couldn't see what was happening from my oblique angle.

I was in time to see Jermaine parry a blow to his face. He was on his knees and trying to get up, the latest assault knocking him off balance again. He rolled backward, pushing off with his hands as they went beneath his head. Up he sprang, but the safecracker had followed, moving fast for such a big man.

A two-handed shove sent Jermaine reeling.

Anna and Georgie thrashed in my arms, wanting to get free so they could join the battle. It took all my effort and quite a lot of rude words to keep them aloft.

The running footsteps outside skidded into a tight turn to get into my suite.

"Halt!" commanded Lieutenant Heather Jacobs, breathlessly aiming at the giant's centre of mass. "Ship's security! We will fire!"

They both had their guns drawn when they raced by me, but neither got a shot off.

The safecracker's response was to launch a chair at them. Not a dining chair that might weigh a handful of pounds, but an armchair that matched the couches. It was so big, it was almost impossible to see. I only knew it was coming my way because it blocked out the light from the windows.

It missed me, but hit Lieutenants Jacobs and Stanislav as they ran into the room, bowling them over like pins.

Too stunned to move, I gawped open mouthed at the hulking man glaring my way. He and I were the only ones still standing, but I guess he calculated the odds and decided they were no longer in his favour for he chose that moment to turn tail and run.

I caught a flash of white when his eyes looked my way, then he was gone, running toward the sun terrace. One massive hand snagged the black rucksack full of treasure and he barrelled through the glass of the sliding door without breaking stride.

Jacobs was getting up, groaning with pain as she did. Jermaine and Alistair were also clambering painfully back to their feet, but no one was going to stop the giant from escaping with Finn Murphy's haul of gold and jewels.

A warning shout from Jacobs went unheeded, and the shots that followed missed their target as the safecracker leapt the glass handrail and vanished from sight over the side of the ship.

Fighting for breath and with my heartrate jacked to its maximum, I had to force my feet to move. He'd jumped over the side. We were twenty decks up. It was a hundred feet to the water and the rucksack of treasure had to weigh a couple of hundred pounds. It was gold for goodness sake!

To my great relief, running to the sun terrace, Jermaine and Alistair both joined me, all three of us having to step carefully around the broken glass lest we slice our feet to ribbons.

The splash had been muffled by the sounds of the wind and waves, but the expanding ring where he entered the water was right beneath us.

Lieutenant Jacobs arrived next to me, wincing and holding her left arm awkwardly, she aimed her weapon at the water below and barked into her radio.

"The intruder went over the side. He's in the water on the port side beneath the Windsor Suite. Get a team down there now!"

Alistair held out his hand, requesting she hand over her radio.

"This is the captain," he spoke with his usual calm confidence. "I want every available on duty security officer at the bridge elevator in five minutes. Contact the port authority and have them put boats in the water. We'll need divers too. Make it happen."

He got a 'Yessir,' and handed the radio back to Jacobs.

"You're injured," he observed, noting her clearly broken left forearm. Alistair had blood coming from an open wound above his left eyebrow and from his mouth. I turned to check Jermaine only to find he was no longer there.

In the next second, the lights inside my suite burst into life, stinging my eyes – Jermaine had closed the breaker. I spotted him returning from the lobby area; I couldn't have told you where the fuse box was.

He had blood around his nose, there was an ugly lump on the right side of his forehead, and an angry red welt running across his chest where he'd collided with something.

I couldn't stop the tears that came. "Sweetie, are you hurt?" I asked, twisting at the waist to look at Alistair too for the same question.

"My injuries are superficial, madam."

"Mine too," added Alistair though I was certain they were both playing down how they were feeling. Then it occurred to me that the impact on their egos might be the harder hit. Jermaine wasn't used to losing. I'd never seen it happen, in fact. And Alistair is the captain of the ship. Turning up for work with a bruised face and looking like he'd been involved in a drunken brawl was going to bother him more than the cuts and bruises themselves.

I placed Anna and Georgie on the carpet, finally content they would fuss around me and the people in the room rather than try to escape.

"Shall I make tea, madam?" enquired Jermaine, heading for the kitchen. He was acting as if nothing much had happened, employing that part of him that wanted to live in British Empire times when nothing could ruffle one's exterior and tea at an appropriate time was what kept Britain great.

"I think perhaps a stiff gin is in order, sweetie. Make mine a double and don't hold back on the gin." I got a nod and a smile to acknowledge my request, but I had to then advise, "Please put some clothes on first, Jermaine, and let the medics take a look at your injuries. In fact, I'll make the gins, you go find clothes." To his departing back I called, "And I don't mean full butler garb either. Put something comfortable on!"

Alistair had fetched his own radio from the bedroom and a robe to cover his body. Emerging from the room mid conversation, he came directly toward me, a robe for me folded over his arm. He was liaising with crew and the port authority, local cops, and goodness knows who else, but he paused to plant a kiss on my cheek and make sure I was doing okay.

More security officers had arrived just in time to miss the action. Lieutenant Stanislav, from Poland, was out cold. The airborne armchair had knocked him back into the wall where he'd hit his head. There were medics tending to him.

I made my way to the kitchen, fetching a bottle of Hendricks from a drawer in the freezer and turning to get glasses from the cupboard behind me. With my arm halfway to the handle, I froze.

My handbag was sitting on the counter.

My missing handbag.

Saying nothing, I placed the bottle of Hendricks down and took a moment to rationalise what I was seeing. A bullet had cut through the strap, and it fell to the ground in a dingy Rio backstreet. Now it was in my suite and the only way that could happen was if the safecracker brought it with him.

Why?

With a double thump of my heart, a nightmarish thought arose and got dismissed. While in theory my handbag was big enough to contain an explosive device, I doubted very much that was why he went to the effort of returning it. Also, it looked empty.

With my teeth clenched together – quite what that would do if a bomb went off, I had no idea – I used a fingernail to open it and peer inside.

Jermaine reappeared from his cabin, dressed now in cotton sweatpants and a t-shirt. He spotted the incongruity instantly.

"Your handbag, madam?"

I nodded, skewing my lips to one side. Picking it up, I tipped the contents out. My phone slid out and across the counter, stopped by Jermaine's hand before it could find its way to the floor. It was a relief to have it back, the passport even more so for the headache its return avoided.

To my great annoyance, the slip of paper in which Sam had folded his white powder was missing. It was as if the giant safecracker had chosen to tidy my handbag before returning it. It was baffling. The gold coin was also gone but that came as no surprise.

Alistair raised his voice in reaction to something he was told, drawing my attention back his way.

He looked my way, his face betraying the frustration he felt.

"They found nothing." To further clarify his point, he added, "There's no sign of him in the water. The port authority put boats out and deployed patrols along the quayside. No one has exited the water, and no one is in the water."

"So ... he drowned?"

Disappointment and Surprise

Silvestre was disappointed to see Gomez return without the woman. Patricia Fisher was fast becoming a thorn in his side. Killing people when they got in his way had always been easy, yet this one unassuming, middle-aged woman from England continually defied his attempts.

Gomez was supposed to bring her back with him so Silvestre could extract what she knew. However, the unchecked item on his list had begun to feel like a chore and the unexpected haul of San José booty demanded his attention. He had the treasure now and could move on. If it proved necessary to revisit Patricia Fisher he would do so, but it was no longer his highest priority.

No, he decided, she could live. For now, at least. The treasure required analysis, the dirt and sand he found stuck to it in places might help to pinpoint where it had been for the last three hundred years.

Even though Gomez failed to deliver Mrs Fisher, Silvestre knew it would be foolish to chastise his valet – such a capable assistant would prove impossible to replace.

Escape by means of scuba gear tethered beneath the ship ensured no one could follow and allowed Gomez the clean getaway he needed. Gaining access to the ship had been even easier: Silvestre had bought him a ticket.

Dismissed for the night, Gomez had retired to his room leaving Xavier Silvestre to pore over the three-hundred-year-old treasure. He could not believe his eyes.

There was so much of it and yet he knew it was a tiny fraction of the booty to be claimed. He needed to know where the rest of it was hidden. Were he to come forward with what he had, not that he would, he would be asked to reveal where it had been found. Finn Murphy knew, did Patricia Fisher?

In all honesty, Silvestre doubted she did. He could not, however, rule it out and that was why he had to question her. Killing her would be easy. If he could be sure she knew nothing, he could kill her and be done with it. Gomez claimed to have fought her bodyguard and reported an easy victory.

The news came as no surprise though, Gomez suffered from Cipa - Congenital Insensitivity to Pain and Anhidrosis – a rare medical condition whose sufferers were unable to sweat or feel pain. So far as Silvestre understood, the condition did nothing to reduce a person's life span, but the inability to feel pain was something to do with nerve endings. It meant Gomez would fail to notice a mortal wound if he ever suffered one and would quite literally bleed to death without feeling the cut.

To that end, he had taken it upon himself to check his valet over when he returned. He had a few bruises, but nothing that mattered.

Turning his thoughts back to the gold, Silvestre once again found himself fantasising about where the crew of the San José had stashed it all those years ago.

Forming a Theory

"A top up, madam?" Jermaine's enquiry broke through the bubble of thought I'd lost myself in and a good thing it did too. The giant had come close to hauling me off the ship and I don't mind admitting that I was shaken. The bustle of people in my suite would be unwelcome at any other time – I ought to be sound asleep in bed at this hour – yet right now I was glad for their intrusion.

It gave me something to focus on. With Jermaine's support, I handed out hot drinks and made people feel like they were guests. They were distinctly more welcome than the safecracker.

Alistair had called the on-duty security officers to deal with the aftermath of the fight in my suite and I chose to let my team sleep. Baker, Schneider, and everyone else would have plenty to keep them busy when the sun rose, so there was nothing to be gained by involving them now.

The dogs buzzed around, excited to have so many new people to meet. More than that though, they expressed their confusion about the lack of breakfast. They were up, the humans were up, therefore it had to be time to eat.

I assured them it was not the case and got barked at for my efforts.

Photographs were taken, fingerprints lifted, and statements recorded. That it all occurred under the critical eye of the captain meant actions were efficient and jokes were non-existent. Despite their expediency, by the time they were done, and I could realistically return to bed, it was too close to morning for me to bother.

Jermaine continued to assure me that he was not badly hurt. Alistair claimed no different. The medics tended their cuts and grazes, using two steri strips to close the wound above Alistair's eye. Otherwise they both acted as though they were fine.

When the bulk of our visitors had departed, and two chaps from the maintenance team had arrived to place a temporary patch over my broken patio door, I ventured a question about the fight.

"Do you think he might have taken something? Drugs I mean," I posed it to both Jermaine and Alistair, getting quizzical expressions from them both. "I mean, I saw you both land blows," I meant Jermaine really, but I wasn't going to insult Alistair by not including him; he fought valiantly, "and they didn't have any effect."

Jermaine skewed his lips to one side, his eyes cast down in thought.

Alistair said, "I'm not so sure I landed more than one good punch, but you're right, at the time I thought it was good enough to have knocked him on his butt. It sure hurt my hand."

Jermaine agreed. "I got a few hits in … decent strikes. It was like he couldn't feel them."

No one said anything for almost a minute, the silence broken when I said, "He came for the treasure. He knew I had it, but I don't see how he could have known it was in my safe."

Alistair shook his head. "There's a safe in every cabin on this ship. Obviously, most of the cabins have a tiny one located in the bottom of a closet, but it's not a big stretch to assume there would be one here. If he knew you had the treasure, then he knew to look for a safe. My question is how could he have known?"

Ah. I hadn't gotten around to telling him that part yet.

"We lost one of the coins," I admitted, expanding my story to include the fight after we tailed Inigo and the part where we got shot at. I kinda smudged over the part where Barbie stole a car. It might have been justified, but Purple Star employees are expected to act as ambassadors of the firm everywhere they go. Breaking laws when ashore is a fast way to get oneself dismissed.

Alistair had some choice words to say anyway. Not aimed at me exactly, more sort of raging to the sky about how often I find myself in perilous situations.

Opting to distract him from asking me more questions, I took out my phone.

"Look, I remain convinced ..." I thought about the cocaine, "mostly convinced that this is all about the treasure. The stowaway's body was the start of it. You saw the information about the San José, and I think it's safe to assume Finn Murphy found it. Somehow the leading academic authority on the subject got involved. I have literally no idea how, but it cost him his life. Professor Noriega was murdered despite what the coroner's verdict might say, and so too was his research assistant. Yesterday someone killed Hector Benzali, who just happens to be involved with Professor Noriega's daughter. It's all connected."

Alistair eyed me suspiciously. "What are you saying?"

"That the man who came at me with a knife on the British Union Islands and the man who broke in here to get the treasure tonight are linked to Finn Murphy's murder. I don't, however, think either one of them did it."

"Why not?" he challenged.

I thought about trying to explain the itch I always get at the back of my skull, but chose to go with, "Just trust me." He rolled his eyes but didn't argue. "They didn't kill him and I'm not saying they are working together, but they probably know who did."

"Yes, well, there's no good reason to pursue it any further, Patricia. It's time to let this one go. Finn Murphy's body was repatriated back to Ireland when we docked yesterday. You can't solve them all."

I was aghast. My mouth hung open. "I jolly well can." Honestly, it wasn't my ego speaking, it was the need to have answers. I'd only been at this job a short while and Finn Murphy was the first murder to occur on board during my tenure. How would Purple Star view their little ship's detective experiment if I couldn't solve a murder? Reaching out to place a hand on Alistair's arm, I spoke in soothing tones. "We need to know if it is over. I have more than twenty-four hours to figure out who killed Hector Benzali and why. If I can do that, maybe I can solve the whole thing."

Alistair wore a pained expression and didn't want to make eye contact. As captain he got to say yes and no as he felt each situation or request required. I was a different and far trickier proposition. He was winding up to tell me not to and I wasn't going to give him the chance.

"I'll take the whole team, darling. I'll be well protected."

He shot me a look. "Against the impervious man mountain we fought tonight? Baker had better take a bazooka with him."

His comment lightened the mood, bringing smiles all round.

"This is the safest play." Picking up my phone again, I went for broke on a wild theory that had been banging around my head since I saw the packing crates on the table next to Hector's body. "Can you read these?" I pushed my phone across to Alistair.

Like everyone employed by Purple Star ... well, everyone but me, Alistair spoke multiple languages. The crew were expected to be fluent in at least one other language, and able to communicate in a bunch more besides.

Portuguese was a doddle for him.

As his eyes fluttered over the words on my phone's tiny screen, reading the lines on the shipping manifest, I did my best to not make my theory sound too outlandish.

"Soooo, Finn Murphy is found aboard a ship. A ship that is heading to Rio."

Alistair looked up. "As well as many, many other places."

"Yes," I agreed, "Stay with me on this. He was bound for Rio, which just happens to be where the world's leading expert on the San José is located. He dies before he can get there, murdered, but the fortune in gold and jewels he is hauling remain hidden. We found them more than a week after his death."

Alistair gave up trying to read and focused on what I was saying. "Go on."

"Well, what if this wasn't his first trip? Someone found out, tracked him down and killed him. They wanted the treasure but didn't get it."

"Our metal detectors would pick it up the moment anyone tried to bring it on board. Their luggage goes through the same scanners one gets at an airport. Exactly the same."

I offered him an apologetic look.

"We both know people can be bought."

I saw his lips twitch, but we both knew there was no way he could argue.

"The San José treasure is worth billions, remember. Not millions. Billions. A few greased palms to make things possible would be no barrier at all."

Alistair gave up. "Okay, so a ... mule? Is that the right word? A treasure mule is carting a fortune in gold and jewels across the world on my ship. Someone else comes on board, finds Finn Murphy and kills him when he won't give up the location of the loot. Finn, running scared and desperate, swallows some of the uncut gems before he died, either because he had them on him and can't figure out what to do, or perhaps because he thinks he can claim he was robbed and keep them for himself."

I spread my arms wide in a 'who knows' gesture. "Let's assume that's the case, but the point is the treasure never reaches its destination. It's heading for the museum where it is being valued and shipped to collectors around the world. Professor Noriega was in on it. So too his research assistant, Antonio Bardem. Both were killed, possibly by whoever is the mastermind behind it all because the 'mule' failed to deliver the cargo – I'm going to assume it was one of many – and they were suspected of stealing it. Sonia knew about her father's illegal activities ... she was probably involved. Her boyfriend, Hector, too. It explains why she looked so nervous when I saw her. She's being leaned on by the man at the top and her boyfriend was killed as a warning. The man who came aboard posing as Professor Noriega wanted to know about Finn Murphy. My guess is that he is the man behind it or one of them at least. The man who broke in here last night could be part of the same organisation or a specialist contractor brought in to steal the treasure back. They knew it was here. How? Because they are the ones running the treasure mules. The best bit, obviously, is that now they have the treasure, it's gone straight to the museum. We can catch them with it and bust the whole thing."

Alistair scrunched up his face. "I don't know, darling, that all seems like a bit of a stretch."

A wolf's grin spread across my face. "It would be if I didn't already know who the trigger man at the museum is."

Jermaine, who had been silent in the background for the last ten minutes, blurted, "Inigo Montoya!"

Alistair flicked his gaze to Jermaine, back to me, back to Jermaine ... With a groan he accepted defeat.

"You're going to bust an enormous underground treasure smuggling ring wide open, aren't you?"

I leaned in to kiss his cheek.

"Yes, darling."

Breakfast and Plans

The manifest turned out to be a list of Roman artefacts – amphoras, pots, things like that. Essentially, it was most likely a red herring and nothing whatsoever to do with the treasure being smuggled. It was bound for the Smithsonian in Washington DC, most likely a transfer of artefacts to be displayed – I remembered the diplodocus that dominated the entrance to the Natural History Museum in London being packed up to go on tour.

Alistair was good enough to go through all the photographs to be sure he hadn't missed anything, and task complete announced he planned to get an hour's shut eye. It was all he had time for. I'd been mainlining coffee to beat back the effects of the industrial strength gin I drank and felt zippy as anything despite the lack of sleep.

To my great surprise, when I crawled into bed next to Alistair, I fell asleep within seconds. Not only that, when I awoke sixty-three minutes later to the sound of his alarm going off, I felt great. It was one of those amazing sleeps where you crash hard, your brain shuts down to the bare minimum activity required to keep you alive, and you get a whole night's worth in a fraction of the usual time.

I almost bounced out of bed.

Almost. I mean, I am in my fifties.

An hour later, with the dogs walked and fed, I was sitting on the couch with my legs curled under me and a cup of tea steaming on the coffee table to my front. Preparing for the day, I fired off a quick message to my team. With a little help from Barbie, I was becoming quite efficient with my laptop.

Everyone's name was listed in a group so I could email them all with just one click. Check me out.

They would join me for breakfast in plain clothes and knew we were going ashore. I would fill them in on the rest of it when they arrived. I included Barbie in my email because I knew she would be disappointed if I didn't. She wasn't part of the security team assigned to me, but with her injured foot, she wasn't instructing in the gym either. If she wanted to join in, she could. The invitation was to Hideki also as I knew he was on call yesterday and therefore had today off.

Anna and Georgie were snuggled in next to me, asleep again now that their bellies were full. I wanted to take them with me today as I hadn't yesterday and felt guilty that I couldn't. They were not allowed in the museum and trying to sneak them in would just cause problems.

Alistair was going to have them in his cabin behind the bridge for the day. He could look after them there and they would be treated like celebrities all day because I knew he would take them into the bridge with him and probably for a walk around the ship because he liked to see the passengers and crew each day.

The message I sent to my team garnered its first reply less than thirty seconds after hitting the send button.

It was from Lieutenant Commander Baker. "Mrs Fisher, I just heard there was an intruder in your room last night! And that he broke into the safe and beat up the captain! Are you all right?"

I hastily typed, "I'll tell the whole team about it over breakfast. See you shortly." I didn't want to have to tell the story ten times in quick succession.

Downing my tea, I patted the dogs, who opened one eye each just to make sure I wasn't going to make them get off the couch. They got an extra neck scratch which made them both close their eyes and lean into my fingertips, then I heaved my backside up and headed to my bedroom.

Jermaine, as usual, had judged my mood and the likely events of the day to lay out three outfit choices. Each was matched with shoes I could run in.

"There will be no running," I told my reflection. "Today will go smoothly. We will snoop on Inigo Montoya, ask some careful questions about Sonia Noriega, and when I am sure I know what is going on and who the persons directly involved are, I will call the police and have them swoop. My team will get the credit they deserve while I will earn a commendation from the people at Purple Star and an oversized gin and tonic."

I went with a pair of bleached denim, skinny fit jeans. They were the sort of garment I would never have felt confident enough to wear a year ago. It wasn't about my size or shape – yes, I've lost some weight since coming aboard, but the change in me had nothing to do with that. A year ago, the jeans would have seemed too attractive, too nice. I wasn't deserving.

That was where my marriage had landed me. Too many offhand re-marks aimed my way by the man I married thirty years earlier.

It was so far behind me it was all but a distant dream ... like something I once read about in a book. Pausing for just a second, I asked myself when I had last thought about my former husband. Okay, so the divorce hadn't been finalised yet, but the paperwork had been signed and I had moved on. So far as I was concerned, Charlie Fisher was my ex-husband.

Weeks, I decided. It had been weeks since Charlie Fisher last crossed my mind. I still carried his name, but only because reverting to my maiden name just felt silly and would involve too much faffing with passports and such. And I would have to constantly correct people because the world knew me as Patricia Fisher.

Pushing him from my mind once more, I slipped out of my robe. From a drawer to my left, I selected a bra that went with the white designer t-shirt I was going to wear, and made sure I had that on before I settled at my dressing table to tackle my makeup.

I was still getting ready when the sound of the girls barking and Jermaine answering the door filtered through – the team were arriving.

Opening my bedroom door resulted in a whoosh of smells to assail my nostrils. Jermaine had been cooking breakfast and was never happier than when he had a host of mouths to feed. My stomach announced its opinion, making a noise like the mating call of a humpback whale and at roughly the same volume.

Bacon. Bacon was the problem. It is always delicious and produces an odour one can never mistake for anything else.

My goodness I wanted some bacon.

I got a round of 'Good mornings' from everyone when they saw me coming their way. They all wanted to know about the safecracker and Jermaine's fight with him. He was being tight-lipped as usual, answering their questions by deferring to me.

Anna and Georgie were underfoot. Unable to resist the smell of bacon, their noses pointed to the ceiling and they were sitting upright like meerkats, sniffing deeply and praying someone would feel a need to feed the poor, starving creatures.

Much to my surprise, Gloria was with Sam. It had been very much my intention that Gloria wasn't to know about the treasure – I had serious doubts that she would be able to keep quiet about it. Unfortunately, Sam talks in his sleep and when his gran quizzed him on the subject of gold and jewels in my safe, he cracked like an egg. So far, though, Gloria had not told anyone else so far as I could discern.

"Are you planning to come with us today?" I asked. "Not spending the day with your friends?"

"Nah, they're all right, but they wanted to look around a gallery and then visit a cathedral. It was boring."

"I'm afraid we are going to a museum," I replied, hoping I might put her off. I have nothing against Gloria, but she can be a mite unpredictable.

Sam's gran cackled, "Yeah, but with you there it will probably explode or something. I don't want to miss that."

I wanted to complain, but everyone else in my cabin acted as though she was making a fair point.

To get away from the subject of my ability to attract trouble, I told them what they wanted to know about the incident with the giant in the night – I had no particular wish to relive it in detail, so they got the edited version. However, they needed to know to look out for the seven-foot giant, not that I could give them a good description – the lights were off the whole time. I also wanted them to understand my theory about the connections between Finn Murphy and everything that had transpired since.

"How much of that is guesswork, Patty?" Barbie wanted to know.

I gave a one shoulder shrug. "Most of it. I cannot claim to know anything. Yet it all fits."

She swallowed what was in her mouth, washed it down with some coffee, and fired off her next question.

"So what are we doing today?"

Martin echoed her, "Yeah. We are all involved in this." He cast his eyes around the table to see if anyone would argue. "What's the play?"

With a nod of my head, I finished my breakfast – a full English with all the trimmings – and set my plate aside.

"I'm heading back into Rio. Back to the museum. Inigo is at the centre of this, we saw that yesterday. It's probably safe to assume he saw us tailing him yesterday and sent the four men in the utility truck to scare us off. I doubt he will be expecting to see us back today. For that matter, I don't want him to see us, so ideally someone new will be following him."

I looked about for a volunteer.

Lieutenant Anders Pippin shot his hand to the sky.

"I can do that."

With a smile of thanks, I said, "You ought to have someone with you. Perhaps, Molly?" I suggested teasingly. "A young man by himself might seem out of place. A young couple though ... you will just look like tourists."

Molly shot Anders a cautious look.

"But we're not a couple," Anders blushed, lying.

I say lying, but relationships are fickle things that are hard to nail down or define. Maybe they didn't consider themselves to be a couple; they were still ever so young. Regardless, they wanted to keep it under wraps, and I wasn't helping.

"Nevertheless, I think the two of you will look natural together. Anyone feel there is a better partner for Anders today?"

No one saw a need to disagree.

Barbie nudged Molly with her elbow and grinned. "Just remember to hold hands and stuff. That way you'll look more convincing."

With a whole bunch of us heading to the museum, we had the opportunity to split into pairs or small groups. More ground would be covered, more questions would be asked.

It was just after eight o'clock. If we wanted to be at the museum when Inigo arrived and make the most of our day, we needed to get moving.

Back at the Museum

Disembarking via the royal suites exit, eleven of us piled into three of the cruise line's limousines. Rio de Janeiro was yet another destination I was visiting for the first time and yet not getting to explore. Alistair was busy with a bunch of essential captain's tasks, but I had plenty of friends and could have spent a full two days ashore. Instead, I was stuck trying to solve another mystery.

Sighing, I watched through the window as the Rio skyline went by outside and not for the first time, made a promise to return when I was not on the trail of a killer.

The limos dropped us around the corner from the museum to avoid drawing too much attention. From there, we split up, the group dividing into smaller parties. Anders and Molly, armed with a photograph of Inigo, downloaded from a social media profile Barbie assured me had to be fake, crossed the road to sit at a bus stop. From there they could watch. Martin and Deepa, a real-life couple, joined the queue of people waiting to buy entry tickets. So too Barbie and Hideki, hanging back so there would be people between the couples.

I was heading for the same entrance as yesterday accompanied by Sam, Jermaine, Gloria, and Schneider. My destination was Professor Baccarin again. Yesterday's conversation got cut short by Hector's murder, but I had all new questions for him today. I wanted to know about Inigo, but I also wanted to look into the professor's eyes when I asked him about the treasure being smuggled into the country via mules and out again through the museum.

My itchy skull told me he wasn't involved, but I'd been wrong before and needed to be sure.

However, with my plan in place and a clear task by task list of what I wanted to do, it all went to pot when we turned the corner and found Captain Santoro smoking a cigarette outside the museum staff entrance.

Two squad cars were parked just across from him, and I could see he was talking on his phone, his right hand gesticulating in the air as he did to leave a swirling trail of blue smoke.

As before, he was in uniform and looking stressed.

Gloria kept on going when I stopped, taking Sam with her as she had a hand hooked into his elbow.

Ducking back to stay out of sight – if Captain Santoro knew I was here again, any chance of investigating would be lost – I hissed at her.

"Gloria! Gloria! GLORIA!"

Sam twisted around to look at me and stopped walking.

Gloria kept on going, only stopping when she got to the end of Sam's reach. Finally, she checked behind.

"What are we doing?" she enquired, looking a little confused. "I thought we were going into the museum to talk to a wizard or something."

Blinking, I shook my head. "A professor. Not a wizard."

"Is there a difference?"

"Quite a big one actually. Anyway, we can't go in if the police are there. We'll have to go around to the front and find a way through."

Ever willing to argue, Gloria frowned, "I've only just walked all the way around here from the front, Patricia. It's too far to go back. Besides, you're trying to solve a murder, aren't you? Let's tell the police who you are," she suggested brightly. "They're bound to help if they know who you are."

Without waiting for my response, she twisted to look at Captain Santoro and lifted an arm. "Cooee! Cooee! I've got ..." Gloria beckoned for me to join her, urgent motions to get me to leave my hiding spot.

"NO!" I hissed at her. "I already met him. He hates me!"

"Oh. You should really work on your personality, Patricia. You always seem to be rubbing people up the wrong way."

Exasperated, I insisted she come to me and had Sam drag her out of sight. Peering around the corner of the building and through the leaves of a handy shrub, I watched Captain Santoro stare in our general direction for several seconds. When he turned away to resume his telephone conversation, I breathed a sigh of relief.

"We need to avoid the police," I explained to Gloria. "They will ..." I was about to say they would eject us from the building when my phone rang.

I fished it from my bag to find Martin Baker's name displayed.

"Martin?"

"Mrs Fisher, we have a small development. Inigo Montoya just arrived. Molly and Anders tried to follow him, but he went in through the public entrance, flashing his ID to someone as he went. I'm about to go in with Deepa, but I think we lost sight of him already."

I swore.

"There's something else."

Hoping to hear good news, I asked, "What?"

"He arrived with a woman. They talked for more than a minute, then she set off on foot when he went inside. Molly and Pippin went after her instead."

"Good thinking. She's bound to be part of the same operation." A thought occurred to me. "What did she look like?"

"Late twenties, tall and lean, tanned skin with black hair pulled into a ponytail. Hold on I'll send you a picture."

My phone pinged a second later, the message containing a picture of the woman I saw Inigo with in the backstreet industrial unit yesterday.

Thinking fast, I asked, "You said Anders and Molly went after her? She's on foot?"

"Yes. They both got out of a car just down from the museum entrance. They stood on the pavement talking, then went in separate directions."

"Okay. I'm going to send Pippin a message. She is definitely part of this. Good luck and let me know if you catch sight of Inigo." I ended the call and relayed what I knew to Jermaine and the others with me, firing off a hasty message to Pippin so he would know to stay on the woman's tail and let me know if he discovered anything.

"So what now?" asked Gloria impatiently. "I can't stand around all day. Not with my hips."

Seeing no options, I led everyone back around the museum's front façade where we joined the queue of people waiting to get in. The initial glut of overeager early comers had dwindled, making it just a few minutes of standing in line to get to the ticket booth.

The entry fee was a paltry few Reals. I tapped a debit card, and we were in. Now we had to find a way to get through to the back end of the museum where I could hope to find some answers.

"Ooh, look at those," gasped Gloria, drawing my attention to a stand offering mobility scooters for hire. It was positioned just before the turnstile to get into the museum proper, and clearly intended to make exploring the vast building easier for those with mobility restrictions. "I've often thought about buying one of those contraptions. It would make getting around so much easier."

She was right, of course. Lots of the passengers on the Aurelia were in their retirement years and brought such things with them. It made getting around the ship's vast decks an easy proposition and I would often see whole herds of them setting out from the ship when we docked somewhere.

The stallholder, a man in his late forties with a pot belly and a receding hairline, noticed us looking and went for the hard sell.

"Cheapest scooters in Rio. Special discount for ladies. Today only. I throw in collision damage for free, yes?"

Giving not one thought to how much they cost to hire, I simply walked to the man tending the stall and asked Gloria which one she wanted.

"The snazzy purple one, if you don't mind."

I flicked my eyes to the stallholder to find he was already ringing up the hire.

"How fast will it go?" Gloria enquired.

The man turned the throttle, coaxing the scooter forward. "Walking pace."

"How fast is that, young man? I don't walk very fast at all."

Pointing to a small knob set between the handles, he advised, "This is the throttle control. Most people leave it set in the middle which is about six kilometres per hour. You won't need it that high to go around the museum and the battery will last longer at the minimum setting." He twisted the knob between thumb and forefinger, reducing the scooter's speed to its minimum.

Gloria swung a leg over the saddle like she was Mad Max and cranked the dial all the way up to maximum.

Gritting her teeth, she snarled, "Let's see what this sucker can do!" and set off with a dynamic twist of the throttle.

I half expected the front end to leap into the air and for blue smoke to pour from the rear tyres as she burned rubber. Instead, the mobility scooter set off at a sedate pace that could best be described as a fast walk.

With debit card in hand, I was about to swipe it on the man's machine when a little voice in my head made me ask, "You mentioned collision damage?"

The stallholder chuckled.

"I'm serious," I assured him, my expression killing his smile. "I need whatever you have including personal liability. The chances she runs someone over are high."

Anxious to get on with my day a moment ago, I made everyone wait now while I insured Gloria and the *scooter of death* against everything short of floods and earthquakes.

Finally through the turnstile and inside the museum, I looked about for anyone who worked there.

Spotting a woman positioned in the middle of the great entrance hall where she was directing visitors this way and that, I made a beeline for her.

"Hello?" I waved, not making any attempt to speak Portuguese. "Sorry, this is going to be a slightly odd request. I need to speak with Professor Baccarin. Is there a way through to the back of the museum where he works, please?"

Sylvia – she wore a name badge – flashed me a professional smile.

"Of course. What you need to do is go back out through the main entrance, turn right, and follow the building around. There is a staff entrance there with a reception. They will be able to fetch Professor Baccarin down to meet you."

I need to carefully word my response because that solution wasn't going to work for us, but Gloria chose to help instead.

"We're avoiding the police," she revealed, making Sylvia's eyebrows rise. "They will probably chase Patricia on account of her involvement with the murder yesterday." Gloria swung her head around to check with me. "I got that about right, yes?"

Sylvia's eyes were twice the size they had been and were now looking around frantically for security.

I grabbed Gloria's throttle and twisted it, shooting her forward.

"Just her little joke," I faked a laugh and aimed it at Sylvia. "We'll do just as you said, thank you." I was moving fast, hurrying away through the crowd, and had to call my last few words so Sylvia would hear them.

"Gloria!" I hissed. "We are trying to keep a low profile."

"I prefer the direct approach," she replied, swerving around a pushchair and almost running over my foot as she did. "Look." She pointed with a nod of her head. "Where does that door go?"

The sign on it clearly stated 'Staff Only'. It was a safe bet it led through to the academic research areas.

Jermaine leaned in close to my left ear. "Perhaps I should check it out, madam."

I nodded, silently, veering off and forcing Gloria to come with me so Jermaine could try the door without a gaggle of us drawing the museum staffs' attention.

He appeared back at my side a moment later. "It is locked, madam. I could probably defeat the lock; it appears to be a simple key operated mechanism. However, perhaps there will be other doors."

"Yes, I think this is a good idea, but we should move on and find one that is already open." In my head the trickiest part of this was getting through to the academic area. Once there, if we were challenged by anyone, I would reel off the list of names I knew, claim I was visiting o n official business and get them to take me to Professor Baccarin. Or to Professor Geller, the head of the museum, he had been so helpful yesterday.

Schneider touched my arm.

"Where's Gloria?"

The wham sound of something solid hitting a door at speed rang through the museum. The background din of conversation dropped instantly, heads swinging around like they were being pulled by a magnet.

I didn't need to see to know Gloria had just employed her mobility scooter to ram the door and she wasn't visible anyway. On the scooter, her head sat below the average height of those around her, but security were coming her way, pushing through the crowd to see what was happening.

Jermaine reacted swiftly, collecting Gloria and catching up to the rest of us as we made ourselves scarce.

Seeing my pinched eyebrows, Gloria said, "I thought that would work." It was as close to an apology as anyone would ever get.

Hooking a hard left through an archway and along a corridor, we found ourselves in a section dedicated to human evolution.

There were more 'Staff Only' doors, yet they were all locked. After a few minutes, and now in a section displaying geology, I began questioning whether we needed to come up with something new.

I stopped to check in with everyone else.

Barbie answered her phone instantly. "Hey, Patty, did you catch the killer yet?" she asked in her usual energetic manner. I'm not sure if it was her Californian accent, or because she is a livewire of energy, but to me she always sounded like she was ready to go for a run. The question she posed was half joking, half serious.

"I'm afraid not. How are you guys getting along?" She was finding female staff and asking about Inigo – how long he had worked at the Museum, was he single … anything that would get them talking so she could find out more about him and the woman he met earlier. She was playing the role of a woman in town who'd met a really cute guy – Inigo – but believed he was too good to be true. Hoping to play on the shared negative boyfriend experiences of the women she chose to approach, I knew she would get answers.

"Well, Inigo has only been here for three weeks, and he's made quite an impression on the ladies. I haven't spoken to one who didn't immediately know who I was talking about."

This did not come as a shock; he was Hollywood handsome.

"He's got the pick of his women here, but hasn't dated any of them yet, it would seem. I showed a picture of the woman he met outside, but no one knows who she is. She doesn't work here, that's for sure. I also asked a couple of girls about Sonia Noriega. Do you know what they said?"

"No. Go on."

"That there was no way she murdered Hector. No way. They said the two of them had been dating for years and were planning their wedding."

It reinforced what I already believed.

"What did Professor Baccarin have to say this time around? Is he involved in the treasure smuggling, do you think?"

With an annoyed sigh, I admitted, "We haven't managed to get to him yet. The police were outside the staff entrance that leads to his office, and we've had no luck finding an alternative way through."

The moment the words left my lips, the nearest 'Staff Only' door opened, a person on the other side exiting through it. I covered the phone with my hand and flared my eyes at Schneider.

He hadn't seen it, but Sam had.

The woman coming through the door had a tablet in her hand and was clearly in a hurry. I'm not sure if protocol was to make sure the doors shut before they walk away, but she didn't and Sam was able to race to it, stopping it from closing by shoving his magnifying glass into the gap.

"Gotta go!" I blurted into the phone. "I'll call you shortly!"

Unprovoked Attack

S lipping through the door, held open by Jermaine, I had to jump out of the way when Gloria barged through on my heels.

"Make way!" she trumpeted, all but skidding to a stop on the other side.

I clamped a hand over her mouth which she licked in defence.

"Shhh! Please, Gloria. We are not supposed to be back here. Our hope of finding answers is predicated entirely upon being able to speak to the right people. That won't happen if you get us kicked out."

She narrowed her eyes at me. "Patricia Fisher, you are no fun at all."

Ignoring her comment, I asked, "Can I count on you to behave?"

Gloria didn't respond straight away; it seemed she needed a minute to think about her answer.

"If I say yes, can I get one of these," she patted the scooter, "for the ship?"

"Goodness, yes, Gloria." I didn't mention that I had already planned to, given how much more mobile it made her.

With Gloria not only quiet, but trundling along at a sensible pace for the first time since she sat astride her hire scooter, we made our way into the back area of the museum.

Schneider went ahead, scouting the way and pausing at each intersection to see if I knew which way to go. I hoped to spot something familiar, but we had only seen a very small part of the museum yesterday and unlike the public areas, there were no handy signposts or labels to guide us.

Twice we heard footsteps or conversation coming our way and ducked into an alcove or an empty room to stay out of sight. It worked, the voices passing us by without realising we were there.

We were not so lucky on the third occasion.

I knew we needed to find an elevator – Professor Baccarin's office is located on the top floor and stairs wouldn't do it unless we left Gloria at the bottom – hardly a solution. There was a bank of them at the back of the building where I intended to enter this morning, but could I find my way to them?

Believing I might have figured out which way to go when we came across a window and could orientate ourselves, the sound of approaching voices came from the direction we needed.

"Quick, find somewhere we can hide!" I squealed urgently yet quietly.

Sam grabbed a door handle, poked his head inside, and waved for us to follow him.

With the voices coming closer – they were going to turn the corner any second now and see us trying to hide – Jermaine shoved Gloria's scooter backwards through the door and gently closed it behind him.

I held my breath, listening for the voices to pass, and only dared to exhale when they had done so and were twenty feet away again.

From behind me, a voice asked, "Can I help you?"

I shot around so fast it's a wonder I didn't end up with my knickers on back to front. Heart banging in my chest, I found a small, studious looking man peering at me and my friends over the top of his reading glasses.

He was in his sixties, with a touch of silver stubble and nary a hair on his head. The glasses were attached to a string that passed around his neck so he could take them off without needing to put them down.

In his hands he held a book, and it was obvious to anyone he had been silently reading out of sight behind a bookcase when we burst in.

I managed to say, "Um."

"Are you with Professor Facioli?" the studious man asked.

Latching on to his question, I said, "Yes."

Unfortunately, at the exact same moment, Gloria said, "No."

The man blinked, his gaze moving from me to Gloria and back again. "Which is it?"

"We are." I stated boldly.

"We are not," Gloria answered, speaking again at the same time as me.

"I think perhaps I should call security," the man remarked, eyeing the imposing forms of Schneider and Jermaine.

Panic stole across me, chilling my blood and making my head feel too light. What was I supposed to say at this juncture? What could I do? Deploy Jermaine to knock the man out? Hardly fair and it would be criminal.

Thinking fast, I was about to ask that he call Professor Baccarin instead when I saw Professor Geller pull up outside. He was more than a hundred yards away but his shock of red hair made him easy to spot.

Professor Geller drove a rather nice, brand new, white Aston Martin, a car that screamed 'I've got money and taste' in pretty much any language. He was getting out of it, and had been visible even when driving because he had the convertible top down.

"Professor Geller," I stuttered, pointing through the window behind the studious academic. "There's no need to call security. My apologies for the subterfuge, I'm here investigating the murder of Hector Ben-zali. Professor Geller hired me," I lied, "and it's imperative we keep my presence quiet."

Seeing a cue, Jermaine stepped forward with his phone screen toward the man.

"This is Patricia Fisher," Jermaine said, his tone serious. He'd selected an internet news article about the Godmother. I don't like that my face is splashed all over the internet, but it does have its uses every now and then.

The man had moved to his desk, at least I assumed it was his desk. A name plate sitting among the clutter declared I was looking at Dr Daniel Fincher. He had the handset of his office phone by his ear and a finger poised to start dialling. He was wavering though, and I pressed home the advantage Jermaine created.

"Professor Geller will vouch for me. You just need to ask him."

"Hey! Where are you going?" the man demanded. Gloria had chosen to leave already. I thought it to be a bad tactic, but actually it was working. Sam went with his gran and when Schneider followed, the man put down his phone to stop them.

I span on my heels, pushing Jermaine ahead of me to get out of the room.

"We're going to see Professor Geller. Please come with us," I invited. I felt confident Professor Geller would be just as helpful today as he was yesterday. Perhaps he would even square things away with Captain Santoro so he would leave me to conduct my own investigation.

Dr Fincher, his reading glasses now dangling from their string as he hustled to get ahead of us, was making sure he would get to Professor Geller first.

"Professor Geller," he called. "Professor Geller."

Coming into the carpark, I looked around for him, but he was nowhere in sight. What I could see was his car. The head of the museum's convertible roof was halfway up and oddly it wasn't moving. He'd been at his car just before we left to intercept him, but there was no sign of him now.

I got a little itch at the back of my skull. What was I seeing? Where had Professor Geller gone? What could possibly have been so urgent that it drew him away when his roof was still only halfway up?

I got my answer in the next second when Dr Fincher squealed, "Professor Geller!"

The head of the museum was lying on the tarmac beside his car, his feet pointing toward us. With my heart in my throat, I clutched at my chest, and grabbed for Jermaine's arm.

Jermaine wasn't there. A moment ago he'd been right by my side, now I had to twist around to find him.

Sensing danger, Jermaine had gone into bodyguard mode. He was only inches from me, but was searching all around for any sign that an attack might happen. Schneider was doing very much the same thing only he was ahead of us.

In the twenty seconds or so it had taken us to get out of the building, someone had killed Professor Geller, leaving his body where it fell. I could scarcely believe it, so imagine my horror when he started to get up.

We were almost at the car where Doctor Fincher, who had rushed ahead to get to his boss, had dropped into a crouch.

"Professor Geller, oh my goodness!" he exclaimed. "What happened?"

Following hard on Doctor Fincher's heels, Sam was with Professor Geller too.

"Mrs Fisher says it's best to stay down if you are hurt," he repeated words I must have said to him dozens of times.

Professor Geller wasn't taking advice though. As the rest of us arrived, he levered himself into a sitting position. He had a cut to his lip where he'd clearly been punched and a graze on his face he might have received when he hit the floor.

"I was robbed," he gasped. "A young man, I think. I never saw him coming."

Doctor Fincher was horrified. "That is unbelievable! I'll call security immediately." He dug in his pocket, came up empty and proceeded to pat his jacket and trousers before groaning. "Nevermind, I'll fetch help." Without another word, he dashed away.

Taking over, I crouched to come down to the professor's level.

"Are you badly hurt?" I asked, looking at his fat lip.

He took a second, refusing to make eye contact which made me think he felt ashamed to be the victim. After a few seconds, he grunted and shook his head.

"No, it's nothing. A cut lip and a scratch."

"You said they robbed you?"

"Yes. I don't carry cash though and my cards can be cancelled long before they will be able to use them."

He was being very mature about it. Too mature even. I've seen people in the aftermath of a violent and unprovoked attack and never has one been this cool about losing their personal things. I wondered if perhaps it was to do with being an academic, like he was able to rationalise everything from a scientific standpoint.

"We really ought to tell the police," I said. "They can take a description of the ... young man, you said? Even if you didn't see his face ..." He waved for me to stop.

"There's really no point," he muttered, sounding tired. "They'll be long gone by now and the security team have enough to do already, what with Hector's murder yesterday." He shifted his feet around, making it obvious he wanted to get up.

Schneider stepped in to offer a hand and I came out of my crouch to give room. Movement to my right, caught in the corner of my eye to make me look that way, showed me precisely what I wanted.

Inigo.

Who to Trust?

I shot out my right arm, angling it toward Inigo's shocked face.

"Jermaine! He's there!" Inigo Montoya was looking right at us, watching from a vantage point inside the building. His expression changed when I pointed his way, shock registering in the fleeting moment before he was gone.

He'd attacked Professor Geller. I didn't know why, yet I was certain that had to be the case. Why else would he be spying on us while the head of the museum picked himself up? He'd just fled the scene, his guilty conscience causing him to check over his shoulder or, in this case, out of a window.

"Do I pursue, madam," asked Jermaine, poised to go, but questioning whether that was the best tactic.

It wasn't.

"No, sweetie. The police are here, and I believe it is time I told Captain Santoro what I have figured out so far." Turning my attention to Professor Geller, I asked in an urgent tone, "What was taken from you, professor?"

I didn't like that there were so many holes in my version of events. I could see why the museum would become the hub for smuggling the San José's treasure, and could piece together enough of the jigsaw for it all to make sense. The players involved though, and where each of them stood; that remained to be determined.

Professor Geller eyed me with confusion. His tie was crooked, and he had dirt and dust on his suit. He was back on his feet though and with the exception of his face, he seemed to be unharmed.

When he didn't answer immediately, I pressed, "Did you have keys to open a restricted part of the museum, or access codes for computers, anything like that? I believe I know who robbed you and we really do have to go to the police, I'm afraid."

I took a pace, indicating to Sam and Gloria that they should angle themselves back toward the museum.

"No, Mrs Fisher," the professor fought me. "There really is no need. Nothing will come of it."

I reached out to take his hand, grabbing it with mine and tugging to get him moving.

"Oh, I suspect that opinion is going to prove wildly incorrect, Professor." I came very close to blurting out that he had a smuggling ring operating under his nose and had to stop myself at the last second. At this stage, telling him anything might put a cross on his back. Instead, as we walked, our pace far slower than I wanted it to be, I asked, "Do you know Professor Baccarin's grad student, Inigo Montoya?"

"The American lad? I have seen him around. Why do you ask?"

"Has he ever approached you or asked you questions?"

"About what?"

I pushed out my lips in a gesture intended to make it look like I was dredging my brain for an example.

"Oh, I don't know. Like maybe he was interested in ..."

Professor Geller wobbled a step, colliding with my shoulder. I stopped what I was saying to stop him from falling and got help from Lieutenant Schneider who darted in to hold the professor up.

Recovering his balance, the professor mumbled, "Sorry, so sorry. I think I should go to my office for a lie down."

I agreed. "I think that's best." With a nod at Schneider – I didn't feel it was a good idea to send the professor by himself - we split up. Schneider kept an arm around the elderly man's shoulders, guiding him into the building as we closed the distance toward two police officers we could see next to the guard hut.

The police had their backs to us. I didn't see Captain Santoro, but that didn't matter – they would contact him on the radio, and he would come. Once he heard them use my name, he would come.

We were fifty yards away when my phone rang. I almost didn't answer it, but glancing at the screen, I saw Pippin's name.

"Anders, it looks like we are sewing things up here. You should be able to stand down shortly. I'm just on my way to talk to the police."

His reply, the way he said it, chilled me to the bone.

"Don't go to the police." It was a command and a warning at the same time, his voice betraying enough fear that my feet stopped moving.

Naturally, Gloria kept going and I had to send Jermaine to stop her.

"What is it, Mrs Fisher?" asked Sam.

I placed a hand on his shoulder and gave it a squeeze, too focused on what Pippin was telling me to answer Sam's question.

"We tailed that woman, the one Inigo met outside the museum. Well, she's a cop, Mrs Fisher. We tailed her all the way to the station. She went inside, so we hung around while we tried to figure out what to do. She came back out ten minutes later, dressed in different clothes and we watched her get into an unmarked police car."

"You're certain," I questioned, my mind reeling from the ramifications.

"I saw her gun and badge, Mrs Fisher." Anders didn't need to spell out the obvious, but he did it anyway, "It looks like the police are taking a cut of the treasure."

The cops were still fifty yards away, but they were looking in my direction now. Two of them; a man and a woman.

I backed up a step, taking Sam with me. Taking the phone away from my mouth, I called quietly to Jermaine.

"Sweetie. Change of plans. We have to go."

His eyes begged to know what had changed and why we were no longer about to speak to the police, but he kept his questions to himself.

Gloria didn't.

"Ere, what's happening now?" she asked.

"Anders, I have to go. It might be best if you head back to the ship with Molly. We'll see you there." The cops were looking harder now, squinting in my direction and arguing about something. I severed the phone call before Anders could respond and dropped it into my handbag.

"Patricia Fisher?" the female police officer called my name.

Perfect. They knew who I was and what I represented – a threat. I thought they were here to make sure they interviewed everyone associated with Hector Benzali. I thought they were trying to solve his murder. They weren't though, they were here to protect their income stream. Whoever Inigo worked for – I didn't think for one second that he was the guy in charge – had paid off the cops. Captain Santoro didn't want me around because I would get in the way and mess with his evidence, but because he was afraid I might figure it out.

"Patricia Fisher!" this time the female cop called louder, wanting me to stop though she didn't say those words.

"They're calling you," Gloria pointed out. "Why are you backing away? I thought we were going to tell them all about the treasure smuggling. Wasn't that the plan?"

I shook my head, taking Sam's hand and gripping it tightly.

"No, Gloria. The police are in on it. If we go to them, they will have no choice but to kill us."

The male cop added his voice, "Mrs Fisher. Stop!" They were coming our way and if we waited any longer, the lead we had would be squandered.

Dropping any pretence, I shouted, "Run!"

Running Defence

I 'm not much of a sprinter, but remember this morning when I was picking my outfit and chose a pair of shoes I could run in? This was why. Right now I was wishing I had also picked out a sports bra.

I took off, catching Sam by surprise so he dragged along behind me for the first ten yards. He's more than thirty years my junior, but he's even less of a sprinter than me, so even once he got his legs moving we were still going slower than I hoped.

Jermaine had no such restrictions. He's not Usain Bolt, but he is a tall, muscular Jamaican man and I reckon he could give a greyhound a decent race. And Gloria, who on any other day would have been someone we had to carry as we ran away, kept pace with ease.

"Told you this thing needed to be cranked up to the fastest it would go," she cackled as she pulled alongside me.

I had no air in my lungs to respond and my thoughts were focused on finding a way to escape. Having gone in search of cops, we were outside the museum, but that meant we were exposed. The only safe play right now was to head back inside. Honestly, I was shocked neither of the cops had chosen to shoot at us. They could give whatever story they liked afterwards, plant weapons on us and say they had to defend themselves. If the cops were on the take, maybe they would just make our bodies disappear.

Jermaine angled toward an open door, increasing his pace to get there ahead of us. It was propped open by a fire extinguisher and was right by the security guards' control room I noted as we ran by. You might think they would have rushed out to see what the commotion was, but from the sound of it they were too busy watching TV.

The cops continued to shout for me to stop. I didn't look back; I didn't need to, I could tell from their voices they were closing the gap.

Bursting into the building, I felt certain they would be using their radios to coordinate with their colleagues. Other cops or the museum's security team would be descending on our location from multiple directions. To get away we were going to have to get inventive.

Ahead of me, Gloria yelled, "Gangway!" when a hassled looking man carrying an armful of loose cardboard files stepped out of a doorway.

The man had nowhere to go and a geriatric with thrill issues bearing down on him at speed. With a squeal of terror, he ran away down the corridor. Gloria didn't slow down. If anything, I thought I saw her crank the throttle back to its top.

Shouting loud enough that there could be no doubt which way the police needed to come, she bellowed, "Get out of the way!"

We were probably lucky the scooter didn't have a horn.

'BEEEEP! BEEEEP!'

Oh, good. It did.

"Gloria!" Now I was yelling too.

"What?"

"Stop yelling!"

"You're yelling!"

"Only because you are yelling!"

"This feels like a situation where yelling is appropriate!"

"Mrs Fisher!" yelled the cops, their voices carrying through the museum's corridors.

"See?" yelled Gloria. "Everyone is yelling!"

I muttered something unprintable between heaving breaths.

"Patty?" Barbie's voice echoed through the corridor. It originated from ahead of us, the direction we were going.

"Gloria," I hissed as loudly as I dared, but definitely no longer yelling. "Don't answer. Just keep going and please try to be quiet."

I heard her say something and though I couldn't make out what she said, I doubted her reply was a polite one.

Jermaine vanished from sight around the next corner, and I heard Barbie's excited, "Babes!" when she saw him.

Gloria took the corner on two wheels ... okay, she didn't obviously, I'm exaggerating to give you a sense of the white-knuckle race through the ground floor of the dusty, old building. I was right on her tail, no longer holding Sam's hand – I had no breath left for anything other than running – but making sure he was by my shoulder.

Barbie was right ahead of us, still in her wheelchair, and with Hideki holding the handles. They were talking to Jermaine, their eyes cutting to look at me, so I saw them nod and start moving in my direction. She had to duck into an alcove to let Gloria go by, hugging the wall to make enough room.

Barbie grinned as we passed each other. "We're running defence! I'm gonna sack the quarterback!" I wanted to give her a hug or something, a little reassurance for me more than for her, but there was no time.

The police were chasing me and those they had seen me with. The chances of evading them for long enough and finding a way out of the museum that was not barred by police or security officers looking for a group matching our description were low to say the least.

Barbie and Hideki would be fine – no one was looking for them. They would delay the cops on our tail, apologising for getting in the way and making a song and dance out of it to buy us some time.

Then they would head back to the ship – the mission had changed. The only thing on our agenda now was escape. If the police here were part of the same conspiracy to smuggle priceless treasure, or being paid off to let it happen, they couldn't let us leave.

They couldn't let *me* leave.

Infamy. It's not a good thing.

In the distance behind me, I heard Barbie squeal in fright, undoubtedly blocking the corridor bodily as she ... what did she say? Something about grabbing the quarterback's sack? I had no idea what that meant and hoped it didn't match the image in my head.

Believing we had gained some time, I slowed my pace and breathlessly wheezed for Gloria and Jermaine to stop.

"We need ..." *gasp for some air*, "to find somewhere ..." *breathe again*, "to lay low for a while."

Jermaine understood. "Because they will have the exits covered, yes?"

I nodded – that didn't require me to use my lungs.

Gloria beeped her horn, getting a scornful look from me in the process.

"Nah," she argued. "Let's just ram our way out! It'll be like on the movies when the car smashes through the barrier."

I rolled my eyes. Hiring the mobility scooter was one of the worst things I had ever done in my life.

My phone beeped with a text message from Barbie.

'*We tied them up for almost a minute. They set off in your direction again, but at a much slower pace. Let me know when you get out. We're going to wait for you around the corner from the museum. I let Martin and Deepa know they need to get clear too. Where is Schneider?*'

I messaged back, '*Thanks, Barbie. Get out and I'll call when we are able to sneak past security. Schneider went with Professor Geller who we met yesterday. He got mugged in the museum carpark when he arrived for work. I think Inigo did it, but I don't know why yet. I'll message Schneider so don't wait for us, just get back to the ship.*'

I got an, '*Okay, Patty,*' from her and wagered that she would ignore my instruction, opting instead to hang around in case we needed her. She was predictable like that.

With my phone still in my hand, I fired off a quick message to Schneider, '*I believe the police are in on the smuggling op. We just got chased. Make sure Professor Geller is okay, then get out of the museum. Use the public entrance and return to the ship. Everyone is heading there now.*'

Leaving out the part where we were not leaving immediately because it was the four of us the police were looking for, I felt hopeful he would obey. My phone was just going back into my bag when he replied.

'*Understood. See you at the ship.*'

Good. That was that taken care of. Now to find somewhere we could lay low.

"If I may, madam," Jermaine pulled my attention his way. "There are stairs around the next corner. That being true, it seems probable an elevator will not be too far away."

Pushing my legs to get moving again, I said, "Good. Let's go find Professor Baccarin. I still have a bunch of questions for him."

Crime Scene Again

Going to see Professor Baccarin invited the risk of running into Inigo. If needed, Jermaine could pound Inigo into a pulp using one hand. Or perhaps an eyebrow. However, the whole business we had unintentionally landed ourselves in the middle of was about as cutthroat as it got. Inigo would be armed; I was willing to bet on it.

With that in mind, we approached Professor Baccarin's office cautiously. Thankfully, finding it proved significantly easier than navigating the ground floor. Coming out of the elevator, we found a painting on a wall that I recognised from the previous visit.

Using that as a reference point, the rest was easy.

Not that it mattered – Professor Baccarin was not there. Our progress stymied, I paused for a moment to gather my thoughts. What else could we do to stay out of sight that didn't involve hiding in a cupboard?

I wasn't a fan of hiding. Avoiding people, yes, but backing into a broom cupboard somewhere with the hope we would not be found, ensured we would be cornered if a search took place. I chose to use my time gathering evidence instead.

"The packing room," I stated boldly. "Where Hector was killed. If there are no police there," I didn't think there would be - they would have finished the forensic examination many hours ago, "then we can get in and have a better look for ourselves."

No one argued, so moving cautiously while also attempting to look like we had every right to be there, we set off. Yesterday, we ran to find the room where Hector was killed, following a pair of security guards. It turned out that meant we didn't actually know the way.

It took us three attempts, but eventually we fetched up in the right hallway. As predicted, there were no police present. The door was covered in yellow police barrier tape, only it didn't have 'Crime Scene' on it but something in Portuguese that I couldn't read.

I knew what message it intended to impart though and yanked it out of the way, nevertheless. I mean, we were hip deep in the doodoo already. Ignoring a police caution hardly mattered when the police are already planning to kill you.

Inside, things were much as they had been the previous day though I could see where the crime scene team had been. Hector's body was gone, obviously, but a grisly stain remained where it had been.

Most notable was the absence of the packing boxes. The bench where Hector had worked in the moments before his death was now clear. No trace remained of the packing lists I photographed or the crates the artefacts were being shipped in. On the floor a yard away, a sole polystyrene peanut lay forlornly by itself, forgotten when everything else was removed.

From one corner of the room, Sam said, "It's not here now."

I swivelled around to meet his eyes.

"The cocaine," he explained, pointing to the floor. "It was right here yesterday."

Gloria said, "Cocaine? I've always wondered about drugs. Would cocaine be good or bad for my angina?"

I pursed my lips. Someone had tampered with the crime scene. In the period between leaving yesterday and arriving now, someone had been in here to clear evidence away. Who did it was relatively obvious – the police themselves were involved. Inigo and whoever he worked for were not content to have Hector's murder interfere with their operation. Who had killed Hector? That remained a mystery, for it could not have been Inigo's people. They would have killed him elsewhere, surely. Why had he been killed at all though?

Taking care, and insisting Gloria remain in the corner by the door, Sam, Jermaine, and I tossed the room once more. We had barely a minute yesterday and had to hurry. Today we got to take our time.

Not that it made any difference. There were no pieces of treasure here – I'd said a small prayer that the black rucksack of loot taken from my safe might be stuffed into one of the cupboards. It wasn't, obviously, but I wasn't upset that God chose not to answer that particular prayer; I know he doesn't work like that.

Whether the white powder Sam found had been drugs remained to be proven one way or the other, for there was no trace of it now. Nor was there any sign the room had ever been used to pack artefacts into crates. There were no packing lists, no crates, no peanuts, and above all no Roman artefacts.

The dinosaur fossil swam back into my consciousness, invading my thoughts like it considered itself to be important. A dinosaur fossil. What the heck did that have to do with anything?

A spark flickered inside my head, fizzing out as I focused on it, then bursting more fully to life as I worked out what the dinosaur bone was for.

The treasure was being smuggled into Brazil to the museum where a team of knowledgeable academics were selling it off piece by piece. Or something like that – the details hardly mattered. To get it out of the country, they were sending it across the border hidden inside crates listed as museum artefacts. If border officials ever opened a crate, they would find what they expected. The treasure would be hidden under a false panel within the crate or something like that.

I could see it all in my head. The Roman things were going to the Smithsonian in Washington, but the dinosaur bone could have been on its way to the Natural History Museum in London for all I knew.

As a method for illegally shipping priceless antiquities, it was genius. The cocaine, which had been throwing me until now because it seemed like such an outlier to everything else, slotted into the same plot. If you have an undetectable method for smuggling things, why not branch out into drugs too.

It was all figured out in my head, but I couldn't go to the police. Back at the ship, if we made it safely there, I could contact Interpol or the FBI – I figured the items going to Washington would get them interested and justify their involvement.

Okay. I said it out loud to myself. "Okay."

"Madam?" Jermaine stopped what he was doing to look my way.

Starting for the door, I announced, "It's time to go. I figured it all out. If we can get out of here, we can bring the whole thing down."

We left the room and didn't bother to put the crime scene tape back in place. From where we were, it was a straight shot back to the elevators we rode when we first arrived. They would land us back in the lobby by the staff entrance. There was a reception desk there and there would be people. If the police tried to grab us, we would scream blue murder.

As a plan it was fraught with risk, but it was all I had, and we had to get out of the building to achieve anything. Sure, I could make calls from where I was, but I didn't have any numbers and the longer we hung around at the museum, the more likely it was that we would get caught here.

We got to the elevator without seeing another person. We heard a few, but they were in their offices working or whatever.

Jermaine thumbed the call button, but the car was already in motion, heading our way. My heart thumped in my chest, beating faster than it ought to. I was nervous, nothing more. In sixty seconds we would be out of the museum and on the streets of Rio. Seconds after that we would be in a cab and home free.

The elevator arrived, pinging to announce itself and the doors swished open.

Inside looking out were the two cops from earlier, the man and woman who ran after us.

Seeing my terrified expression, the man slapped a hand to hold the doors open and both cops grinned like they had just won the lottery.

Famous

"Patricia Fisher," the male cop gasped, his smile impossibly widening even further.

The woman stalked forward, her feet moving faster than they needed to. I glanced to my left at Jermaine. He looked relaxed but I knew he was about to strike. He would disable both cops the instant he saw them go for their guns.

"Oh, my goodness!" the woman squealed, her cheeks turning bright crimson. "I can't believe it's you!"

I felt the planet shift under my feet. What was happening right now?

The man bounced out of the elevator like a child who'd eaten too much sugar. He came right for me but there was no suggestion violence was about to ensue. In fact, he looked like he was going to hug me.

His female counterpart snagged the sleeve of his shirt, holding him back before he could get to me.

"Bruno, remember consent!" she chided him. "She's famous and we are fans, but that doesn't mean you can just grab her. Why do you think she ran from us earlier, dummy?"

Fans? I heard it right, but I was completely thrown.

"I'm sorry, Mrs Fisher," the male cop gushed. "I'm just so excited to meet you. We knew ..." he indicated his partner, "Jordana and me, that is, knew your ship was coming to Rio, but we never imagined we would see you."

Jordana revealed, "We wanted to be at the docks when everyone disembarked. We thought we might catch a glimpse of you, maybe ask for your autograph and a selfie, but our shift rotation denied us the chance."

"But now. You. Are. Here!" Bruno's voice went almost hypersonic in his excitement.

I was reeling, my head feeling light and as if the floor beneath my feet were spinning. They chased us earlier not because they wanted to kill me, but because they wanted to get my autograph.

Like a slap to the face, I realised what this did to all my theories.

Bruno had fished out his phone and had Jordana checking his hair. Backing toward me and checking over his shoulder, he lined up to get a selfie.

Snapping back to reality, I threw my arms in the air. "Wait, wait, wait."

The cops froze, each checking the other to see if they knew what was happening now.

"What about the smuggling operation?" I demanded to know.

The cops looked at each other again.

"Smuggling operation?" Jordana repeated my words like she was trying them on for size.

I found myself momentarily lost for words.

"You cannot be serious!" my mouth hung open and I gawped. "Hector Benzali was killed because he was involved, voluntarily or otherwise, in an operation using this museum to smuggle drugs and priceless treasure out of Brazil. Are you seriously telling me you don't know that?"

Yet again, Bruno checked with Jordana and vice versa.

"Oh, come on" I begged. "What happened to all the evidence in the room where Hector was murdered? Yesterday it was full of wooden crates which Hector was filling with Roman artefacts bound for the Smithsonian. I saw the packing lists." I yanked out my phone to show them the pictures. "And Sam," I indicated my assistant, "found white powder on the floor which I suspect was cocaine."

Seeing that I was being serious, Bruno asked, "You were able to collect some of the cocaine?"

"Yes," I replied, my joy at getting them to listen short lived when I had to add, "But we lost it. It was there though." I paused for a beat, arguing in my head about what I could and could not, or perhaps should or should not tell them. There were corrupt police involved in the smuggling ring, yet these two were not part of it. I guessed that was due to their low rank.

I wasn't going to tell them everything and I certainly wasn't going to accuse their colleagues without concrete evidence in my possession. I knew the police were involved somehow – Inigo meeting with the woman who turned out to be a detective proved it, but that didn't mean all the cops were dirty. I doubted they were. It would be a small, select group who were on the take.

Nevertheless, Bruno and Jordana could be playing me; acting like gushing fans so I would drop my guard and tell them all I knew – something the higherups would want to know before they silenced me. I chose to trust them despite my deep-rooted concern because I had to trust someone.

Treading carefully, I said, "There is a man here going by the name Inigo Montoya. That name is almost certainly fake. He works for Professor Baccarin, who in turn worked alongside Professor Noriega, arguably the world's leading authority on sunken treasure ships." I avoided giving them the name of the ship in question. "Professor Noriega was murdered. His death was recorded as an accident because he was hit by a car, but trust me, he was murdered. His assistant was also murdered, stabbed in a Rio backstreet just a day before his boss died. Yesterday, Hector was killed, his death staged to look like a suicide. He was dating

Professor Noriega's daughter. I'm not going to tell you everything; you will have to extend me a degree of faith. But let me assure you, this is all to do with a multi-billion-dollar treasure find. The kind of money a lot of people will kill for. Inigo Montoya is involved, and you need to catch him as soon as possible."

Bruno swivelled around on his heels to look at Jordana.

She nodded her head at him. "You know what this means, Bruno?"

Bruno emitted a high-pitched squeak. "We get to help Patricia Fisher solve a case!"

"Oh, dear Lord." Gloria slumped on her scooter, exaggerating the motion to make it look like she had fallen asleep out of boredom.

With Bruno vibrating with so much excitement he couldn't manage to think straight, Jordana asked, "What do you need us to do?"

Lies and Subterfuge

We led Bruno and Jordana, otherwise known as Officers Oliveira and Nordin, to Professor Baccarin's office. He still wasn't there, but that didn't matter so much now.

"You believe Professor Baccarin is involved in the smuggling ring?" Bruno asked.

I nodded thoughtfully. "I know Inigo is, so his position as Professor Baccarin's grad student makes sense. Also, I know the professor has intimate knowledge of the antiquities at the centre of this case."

Bruno squeaked again, "Eeeeek! This is so exciting! So much better than what we usually have to do."

Equally star struck, Jordana asked, "What are we looking for?"

"A black rucksack about this big," I held my hands apart, "by this big. Gold coins. Old pieces of jewellery ... basically, anything incriminating."

The door was closed though, and even if it wasn't, the cops couldn't just choose to search it without a warrant – that would render anything they found inadmissible as evidence.

"Are we going in, or what?" asked Gloria, impatient as ever for there to be action.

I pulled a face and looked at the cops. They were treading a line between wanting to help me because of who I am and getting themselves into hot water by doing things they knew they shouldn't.

Jordana was first to cave. "We can't go in there," she stated, her comment aimed more at Bruno than anyone else.

"Well, I can," growled Gloria like she was Bruce Willis about to storm a fortress.

I put my foot in the way of her scooter and reached out to try the handle.

"There's no need to ram the door open, Gloria." I pointed out. I didn't know if it was locked or not, but I wasn't going to have Jermaine kick it open if it was closed. I wanted to look around inside, but breaking down doors in front of cops I wasn't sure I could trust sounded like a bad plan.

The handle turned and the door opened. I got an annoyed harrumph from Gloria as I stepped across the threshold and turned to warn her, "No breaking anything. In fact, no touching anything." Thinking better of it, I pulled Sam across to block her access. "Actually, you should just wait outside. Jermaine and I will handle this."

Gloria blew a wet raspberry at me to an accompanying hand gesture – she was such a delightful old lady.

Professor Baccarin's office was just as we last saw it. I looked around. There was a lot of territory to cover. From my handbag I produced a set of gloves, the thin rubber ones that stop a person leaving fingerprints everywhere.

Jermaine came past me, reaching into a pocket from which he produced a small microphone.

Gloria's eyebrows hiked up her head. "He's going to sing?"

Jermaine moved across the room. Holding the microphone at arm's length, he wafted it here and there, bringing it into close proximity to various objects.

I explained what he was doing.

"A live microphone emits a strong magnetic field. That field, if it comes into contact with a listening device, a bug, if you will, will react by creating feedback through the microphone."

At the exact moment I finished speaking, the microphone began to buzz. It was a deep, angry bass noise that faded in and out and grew in both volume and intensity as he brought it nearer to whatever device was creating it.

Much like using a metal detector, he only had to zero in on the focal point of the noise to find the 'bug'.

Officer Jordana Nordin shook her head in disbelief. "I have got to quit this job and become a private investigator. That has got to be the sexiest thing I have ever witnessed."

I thought about firing off a flippant comment like, "It's just Tuesday for us" but doubted I could pull it off without sounding ridiculous.

Jermaine switched off the microphone, placing it back inside his pocket before lifting a lamp from Professor Baccarin's desk. Turning it over, he plucked a small device no bigger than a fingernail from under the lamp's base.

Gloria asked, "What does that tell us?"

"That someone was listening in. Someone felt Professor Baccarin was worth spying on. Other than that, nothing much at all."

We searched drawers and cupboards, and I had Jermaine glance over some of the paperwork on the professor's desk. Less than five minutes later, I called it quits. There was no black rucksack full to the brim with a fortune in treasure. Nor did we find any evidence linking Professor Baccarin to the smuggling operation.

Finished in Professor Baccarin's office, we backed out to the hallway outside.

"So what now?" asked Bruno.

"Now we need to find Inigo Montoya. I'm still trying to figure out who is involved, but I know he is for sure."

Bruno used his radio to enquire about Professor Baccarin's American grad student. The other police at the museum today, led by Captain Santoro, were questioning staff in what I had formerly assumed was a fake investigation into Hector's staged suicide.

If some or even any of the police here today were working with Inigo – and I was ready to bet they were – then asking them to be on the lookout for him ran the risk of tipping our hand. Equally, if he ran from the police or opened fire ... or anything, it would strengthen my case when I was able to get hold of someone in authority I felt I could trust.

Until I met Bruno and Jordana thirty minutes ago, my only plan was to get back to the ship. Now, though somewhat hesitantly, I was questioning if maybe there was still a chance to score a win, but all the lies and subterfuge were making my head spin.

I heard when the reports came back to Bruno that Inigo had not been seen. More pertinently, I heard Captain Santoro when his voice came over the airwaves.

"Oliveira, why are you and Nordin not at your posts? And who is this Montoya person you are suddenly so interested in?"

Bruno's cheeks coloured, panic rising as he fought to think of an excuse.

I flared my eyes at him, reaching for his hand to delay his reply.

"Do not tell him I am here," I urged. "He doesn't like me." Keeping my presence secret was one thing, but Nordin needed to give his boss a response.

Jermaine asked, "Madam, is Captain Santoro aware of the attack on Professor Geller?"

It was a flash of inspiration. Made more so because Bruno and Jordana didn't know about it either. That surprised me because Schneider was supposed to inform them when he got the head of the museum back to his office.

"Oliveira!" Santoro barked. "Report!"

Quick as a flash, I told him about Professor Geller.

With a lick of his lips, and a worried expression on his face, Bruno clicked the send switch on his radio.

"Sir, we left our posts to investigate a report of assault and robbery." He released the send button, holding his breath.

"You are talking about Professor Geller?"

"Yes, Sir. I see you already know about it. A member of staff reported it to us saying they had seen a man running into the museum. We have not been able to locate him so far and were on our way to check the professor before returning to our posts."

"There's no need to check the professor. I spoke with him myself not more than ten minutes ago. De Souza and Buzolin will take his statement. Do not leave your posts without radioing first. Is that clear?"

Bruno grimaced. He'd just lied to his boss. "Yes, Sir."

Lowering the hand holding the radio, he looked at me.

"What do we do now?"

"Aren't you returning to your posts?" I questioned my understanding.

Jordana replied first, "No chance. This is way too much fun."

Bruno agreed, "Besides, didn't you just tell us there is a drugs and priceless jewellery smuggling ring operating under our noses here at the museum? If you are about to crack that case, you need us around to make the arrests, yes?"

I flicked my gaze between the two cops; they both wanted to disobey their boss and be part of my team for the day. They were looking at me like a pair of hopeful puppy dogs. I mean, I'm sure helping me take down a smuggling ring sounded better than anything else they could be doing. When I first saw them, they appeared to be hanging around outside the back entrance to the museum managing the traffic coming in and out.

With a shrug, I said, "Okay." Having two cops with me wasn't a bad thing. They were armed for a start, and I did need them to perform arrests if we were able to find Inigo or whoever was working with him.

In fact ... "Guys, have you got access to a car?"

Empty Premises

Getting Bruno and Jordana to not only not return to their posts but to leave the museum grounds entirely ought to have been difficult to achieve, yet their fandom level had them excited to the point that they were ready to do almost anything I asked.

Not only that, they were full of questions about the ship, my job, our adventures, the Godmother, which was of course the case that really propelled my name into the limelight.

The Rio police had a small minibus with them today, transport to get a bunch of cops from the station to the museum, I guess. Bruno repurposed it, employing it as our adventure bus when we set off to revisit the backstreet air-conditioning place we followed Inigo to yesterday.

Was I worried we might get shot at again? Well, yes, I was in truth, but with a pair of cops in attendance and armed with the knowledge of what to expect, I believed the risk was justified.

"You were shot at yesterday!" Jordana spat her response to my story in disbelief.

Sam grinned at her, "Yes. Jermaine had to beat up four men."

"Only three," Jermaine corrected him. "You took care of the fourth, Sam."

Sam's grin widened massively.

"But you got shot at," Jordana repeated, unable to wrap her head around it. "I've been a police officer for six years and I've never been shot at."

Gloria almost spat out her false teeth with laughter. "Patricia gets shot at most days."

"I do not!" My protest was instant, but seeing three sets of raised eyebrows from Sam, his gran, and Jermaine, I relented, "Most weeks though, I suppose."

Bruno's eyes were on the road ahead, but his face was screwed up as he tried to match what he was hearing to the picture in his head.

"But you work on a cruise ship," he pointed out. "Isn't it all lost children and an occasional stolen purse?"

It was my turn to laugh, a guffaw rising from my belly to burst from my mouth as I howled.

"My goodness, I wish it was." If there was more time, I would have told them about Commander Schooner and his attempt to sink the whole ship, about how many people he murdered in his pursuit of a priceless sapphire. To that I might have added my more recent night-mare: Angelica Howard-Box and her attempt to scupper my entire life. Then there were art thieves, murderous actors, battling rival gangster families ... the list went on.

There wasn't time though because we were pulling into the street where we were attacked less than twenty-four hours ago. It took half a second for me to know we had wasted our time.

The roller door was up for a start and when we cruised slowly by the premises, it came as no surprise that it was completely empty.

"This is the place?" asked Jordana, squinting into the dim interior.

It was stripped bare.

Bruno stopped the police transport and leaving the engine running got out to have a closer look.

I wanted to see too, yet I was more concerned about the mystery figure who shot at me yesterday, so had my eyes trained on the street behind us.

A skinny cat wandered out from under a grime coated car and a discarded candy wrapper fluttered on a breath of air. Otherwise the street was devoid of movement.

A glance at the empty building revealed Bruno returning.

Sliding into the driver's seat once more, he said, "It's been completely gutted, but it's obvious there was some serious tech in there previously."

Jordana tilted her head in question. "How can you tell?"

Bruno checked his mirror and pulled out. "Dust marks on the countertops where monitors and computers were once placed and on the floor you can see where cables ran. Lots of cables. We could have the place dusted for prints, but there's no way to do that without Captain Santoro knowing." He caught my eyes in the rear-view mirror. "Sorry, Mrs Fisher, this is a bust. There's nothing here to find."

I told him that was okay, of course. We were not getting very far and the remaining time we had to find evidence was dwindling. Earlier I had been ready to face Captain Santoro and reveal what I knew so far. I would have done so were it not for Pippin's call and the likelihood of police corruption.

Now I wasn't sure what to do.

A text from Barbie helped to make up my mind.

'Patty are you guys still inside? Are you okay? Do you need us to create a diversion so you can get out?'

I had most of the people I knew caught up in this mess. I had Finn Murphy's murder to solve, that was the original driver that sent me to the museum. That and the appearance of a murderous fake version of Professor Noriega. It wasn't enough to keep me in the game though. Yes, I wanted answers, however I could sense the danger pressing in around us and decided it was time to go.

"Let's get back to the ship," I murmured, repeating the words a second time at a volume everyone would hear.

Sam's eyebrows did a confused dance on his forehead, but he offered no argument. We needed to return to the museum so we could hand back Gloria's mobility scooter. We were probably not supposed to take it from museum grounds, but having left via a back door, it had been loaded into the luggage area of the minibus and taken across town with us.

Naturally, having chosen to play it safe for once and abandon the mystery I was trying to solve, we didn't get the chance to do so.

Nordin's radio burst to life with Captain Santoro's voice. Jermaine translated for those of us who did not speak Portuguese.

"Nordin there had better be an outstandingly good explanation for why you are not at your post," his voice was dangerously calm and quiet. "I've just been informed that the minibus we discovered to be missing from the carpark is all the way across town." The tone of his words was beginning to gather pace and build in volume. "I need to report it as stolen, which is a mite embarrassing as a police captain because, of course," he reached a crescendo, "it cannot possibly be the case that you are driving it!"

Bruno huffed out a disappointed breath and shot a glance at his partner. They were busted and would catch merry hell for helping me. There wasn't a thing I could do or say to make things any better. Telling Santoro I asked them or convinced them would only make it worse for them.

Reaching up to the radio clipped to her lapel, Jordana sucked in some air and replied.

"Sir, we were following a report that might have shed some light on yesterday's murder." Before he could ask what would have been a predictable question, she continued, "A member of museum staff was seen acting suspiciously and was followed to a building that has since been abandoned. Sir, Officer Oliveira went inside and says it was obviously a base of operations for something clandestine. Sir, I think we are onto something. The site needs forensic examination."

Santoro cut her off. "I'm going to stop you right there. A clandestine base of operations? A suspicious member of museum staff ..." There was a pause. "If I find out you are with Patricia Fisher ..."

"We are with Mrs Fisher, Sir."

Captain Santoro spat something in his native tongue and the fact that Jermaine chose not to translate it was all the translation the words required.

"Get back to the museum now. I will be waiting in the carpark. Do not expect to still have jobs tomorrow."

I could feel heat rising off my cheeks. This was my fault. They were volunteers, but I should have known better than to allow them to 'borrow' the police minibus and abandon their posts.

Bruno stared straight ahead, his eyes locked firmly on the road and Jordana kept her gaze turned outwards, unwilling to make eye contact with anyone.

It stayed like that all the way back to the museum, no one able to come up with anything to say to break the uncomfortable silence.

Turning off the road and into the museum's staff carpark, and past the cops who were now standing where Bruno and Jordana were supposed to be, felt like entering an execution chamber. It was all far worse than if Captain Santoro's ire were aimed at me. That I could deal with.

In fact ...

The moment the minibus stopped moving, or possibly slightly be-fore, I grabbed the handle of the sliding door and swung myself out. Bruno's aim had been directly toward his captain, so the man I wanted to speak to was right there when my feet touched the ground.

"Are you in on it?" I spat, my right index finger jabbing the air ahead of me as I advanced on him. "Are you?" I repeated, my voice loud, my tone accusatory.

Captain Santoro had a sergeant standing just to his left and a pace behind, waiting to deal with the two errant officers no doubt. Like his captain, he was looking my way and had no idea what was happening.

Capitalising on the moment of shock my outburst created, I tried my luck.

"You made it necessary for me to employ Officers Nordin and Oliveira. None of this is their fault. It's yours. So my question again – are you in on it?"

I could sense Jermaine to my left. He was poised to react if the cops went for their guns. Bruno and Jordana were whispering to each other in the front of the minibus, wondering what on earth I was accusing their boss of, for I had steadfastly not raised the subject of police corruption within their earshot.

I figured it was fifty-fifty that Captain Santoro was up to his neck in drug smuggling and murder, but if asked which I truly believed, I would say the man was innocent.

His face led me to think I was right.

"Involved in what, Mrs Fisher?" he asked with a slight shake of his head that looked sorrowful and bored more than anything else. "Involved in Hector Benzali's murder? Involved in Professor Geller's mugging earlier?" His tone was flippant and his face amused. Until I replied, that is.

"No, Captain. Involved in the multi-billion-dollar drugs and priceless artefacts smuggling ring taking place at this museum."

Silence filled the air, seconds ticking by and no one moving. To anyone observing, it must have looked like we had all been hit with a freeze ray.

It broke when Captain Santoro doubled over with laughter. It was the second time he'd laughed in my face.

Dutifully, his sergeant followed suit, smirking and chuckling though only because his boss was.

I folded my arms and waited, a pleasant expression fixed to my face lest I cave to my instincts and whack the man on his head with my handbag. Or Gloria's handbag perhaps since she generally carried something heavy in it.

Almost a minute passed, Captain Santoro making several attempts to start a sentence only to lapse into further spasms of hysteria.

Finally bringing himself under control and able to stand up straight, he wiped some tears from his eyes, brushing the dampness from his fingers onto his tunic.

"My goodness, woman."

I do so love being addressed as 'woman'.

"I genuinely thought you were someone to respect. Someone with a keen detective's intellect. A person able to spot that which ordinary folk fail to see. Instead, I discover you live in a fantasy world of super villains and spies." He sputtered some more laughter. "Smuggling ring! That is priceless. Ooh, let me guess ... you think the academics are behind it!"

"They are."

He burst out laughing again and now that he couldn't speak, I started talking.

"Professor Noriega was the world's leading authority on a treasure ship called the San José. It was sunk off the coast of Columbia more than three hundred years ago. The approximate net worth of the cargo is north of ten billion US dollars. It was found and couriers have been bringing the treasure here for it to then be sold on to collectors. They are also smuggling drugs. Cocaine or heroin would be my guess. My assistant" I indicated Sam, "found white powder on the floor in the room where Hector was murdered." Ok, so I was filling in a bunch of blanks and guessing, but admitting that right now would do me no good so I pressed on. "Professor Baccarin's assistant, a grad student from the US called Inigo Montoya, is a link man for the criminal family underpinning the operation. His identity is fake, he was in close proximity to Professor Geller when he was attacked earlier, and we tailed him to an industrial unit in a backstreet yesterday, a unit that was filled with people and high-tech equipment. We were attacked moments after looking through the window and shot at."

Captain Santoro wasn't laughing any longer. His expression did little to suggest he believed anything I was saying, but he wasn't trying to shut me up either.

"That same unit is now stripped bare, the operatives inside undoubtedly moved to a backup location. In Professor Baccarin's office, we found this," I turned to look at Jermaine, holding out my hand so he could give me the bug he found. "A listening device."

"It's true, Sir," Bruno spoke up. "We were there when Mrs Fisher's assistant found it."

"We didn't go in, Sir," added Jordana quickly. "It wasn't an illegal search."

I slapped it into the captain's right palm.

"Is this the sort of thing you believe to be normal in a museum."

Santoro frowned. "There could be dozens of reasons why it was there."

I jinked an eyebrow in his direction, but didn't comment – he knew he was being ridiculous.

Speaking slowly and with great confidence now that I had everyone's attention, I said, "It gets worse. This morning, my team saw a woman liaising with Inigo Montoya. She was also at the industrial unit we tailed him to yesterday, so believing this might help us to understand what was occurring – I ask you to remember we came here seeking answers to a murder that occurred on board the Aurelia – two of my friends proceeded to tail her."

Captain Santoro shifted position, making me believe he was suddenly uncomfortable because he could guess what I was about to say.

"They tailed her to the police station and watched her emerge not long afterward in different clothes but wearing a detective's badge and a sidearm. She is a cop," I clarified unnecessarily. "And that leads me back to the question about who here is involved in the smuggling operation?" I narrowed my eyes at the captain, no further words needed.

He got it. He might not like it, but he could not ignore the listening device he held in his hands or the corroborated story from Nordin and Oliveira. I might not have all the facts, but I knew enough to scare away his mirth.

Nodding to his sergeant, Santoro issued a command. "I want the museum searched. Find me Inigo Montoya."

"There's no need to look for me, Captain Santoro," a new voice echoed across the carpark. It came from my right, over by the museum. Turning to look. I found the man I had spent much of the last twenty-four hours pursuing: Inigo Montoya.

The Last Thing I Expected

Jermaine took two paces, placing himself between me and the advancing suspect as the cops around me all drew their weapons instinctively.

"Keep coming," commanded Captain Santoro, beckoning with one hand.

Inigo did just that, lifting his hands on either side to show they were empty. Partially hidden behind Jermaine, I peered around his side to find Inigo wasn't looking at the police captain, but at me.

Directly at me and he looked really rather angry.

Speaking from between clenched teeth he snarled, "Mrs Fisher, you have no idea the trouble your interference has caused."

If you gave me a pen and paper and asked me to jot down a thousand things he might have said as an opening gambit, those words would never have entered my head.

Coming closer, he finally twitched his eyes to the man in charge and said, "I'm going to reach for my badge."

His badge?

"Slowly," warned the sergeant.

From the back pocket of his jeans, Inigo Montoya produced a small, black leather wallet-looking thing which he deftly flipped open to reveal a badge no one could fail to recognise.

He was FBI.

"I'm here as part of a taskforce tracking the illegal cross-border movement of ancient artefacts. The detective Mrs Fisher's people tailed to your station is my local liaison." He twisted his head to shoot a look my way. "Yes, I've been listening to Professor Baccarin among others. However, thanks to you, my whole operation is blown."

I felt heat rising off my cheeks though I didn't feel like I had done anything wrong. How could I have known?

Captain Santoro had taken the agent's identification which listed his name as Mandy Patinkin, not Inigo Montoya at all. He handed it back now, refusing to look my way when he asked, "So it would be fair to say that Mrs Fisher ruined an expensive FBI investigation and scuppered the chances of catching the people behind the crimes you were investigating."

Agent Patinkin shrugged and sighed, a lungful of air exiting through his nose so he visibly deflated in front of us.

"Actually, no."

Well, that was a relief to hear.

"In truth, we had already concluded there was nothing here to find. Whoever is shipping the artefacts into the US, they are not doing it from here."

"What about the drugs?" Sam wanted to know. "I found cocaine."

Agent Patinkin was kind in his reply, but said, nevertheless, "I highly doubt that. There is nothing going on here."

Staying quiet is not exactly in my nature, but even if it were, I would have found myself speaking now.

"Are you all blind?" I raged. "Hector Benzali was killed while packing Roman artefacts into boxes!"

Agent Patinkin nodded. "Yes, he was. Roman artefacts that the Smithsonian is expecting. I checked the manifests myself. Everything he was shipping was planned in advance and annotated by a paper trail as long as my arm. This is just one museum we are investigating and I'm afraid there is nothing happening here. I will fly back to Langley tomorrow to be reassigned elsewhere."

"So how do you explain the three murders?" I demanded to know.

"This again," muttered Captain Santoro. "For the last time, Mrs Fisher, Professor Noriega was killed in a hit and run accident and his assistant, Antonio Bardem found himself involved in a drug purchase gone wrong. Not every crime that occurs will get you into the papers, I'm afraid," he scoffed as if that could be my only motivation. "I'm sure everyone here read your report on the murder of Finn Murphy and the jewels found in his belly. Was any of that true, Mrs Fisher? Or had you just been out of the limelight for more than five minutes?"

Seething, I was about to argue, even though I knew it was becoming futile, when Agent Patinkin got in first.

"As for Hector Benzali, I believe Sonia Noriega killed him. Working closely with and around them, I have heard their arguments myself. They have been fighting for a week or more. About what I could not tell you, and to be honest, it was not something I gave much thought to until she killed him and staged his death to look like a suicide."

"There you have it," concluded Captain Santoro, daring me to produce evidence that would prove I knew better. "There are no drugs, Mrs Fisher. There is no smuggling ring. The deaths you so desperately cling to are not part of a massive conspiracy." Nodding his head to get his sergeant involved, he added, "Sergeant Braga, escort these civilians back to the port and see that they board their ship."

My top lip twitched; a scathing rebuke hidden just behind it that was only kept in check by the scantest margin. No power on earth would convince me Professor Noriega's death had been anything other than murder, but unless I was going to tell the world about the San José and the safecracker who invaded my suite last night, I had to remain quiet.

Glaring down at me as he held all the cards, Captain Santoro delivered a final threat.

"Mrs Fisher, as previously mentioned, it was made clear to me that I was not to cause an incident that would make the papers. Let me be clear to you now though that if you set foot back outside the port today, I will arrest you on sight. I do not care if you are in a bar across the street having a cocktail, I will arrest you. I will slam you into a cell along with whoever is with you, and I will hold you there for as long as I can. Certainly long enough that I find myself forced to race to deliver you back to your ship just before it sails."

Sergeant Braga held an arm out to guide us back onto the minibus and a small sea of faces looked inward at us. There wasn't a friendly one among them. Bruno and Jordana were looking sheepish, waiting for their boss to carve chunks off them now he was done with me.

I tried to offer them a defiant smile, but they weren't looking my way.

"Are we going now?" asked Gloria. "I've not returned my scooter yet."

Sergeant Braga was not inclined to let anything delay our departure.

"I will see that it is returned," he stated flatly. "Please take a seat."

The ride back to the ship was a sombre one.

Bedroom Intrusion

Staring back at the mountain rising into the sky above Rio de Janeiro, I reflected on how little of the city I had been able to see. I hadn't really seen any of it. Too wrapped up in my need to find answers, I had missed the chance to do what anyone else would have on their first visit to the famous location – act like a tourist.

Heck, I could have taken a book and laid on the beach. I would have achieved about the same amount, and I'd feel a jolly sight better about it.

The minibus pulled through the security gate and into the dock, Sergeant Braga riding shot gun in the front with a junior police officer at the wheel.

Aiming for the ship, they parked a few yards from the line of passengers waiting to board through the main entrance.

Jermaine spoke up, "Mrs Fisher boards through the royal suite's entrance near the prow."

Sergeant Braga didn't bother to consider his reply. "You can walk."

"We have an eighty-year-old lady on board," I pointed out. "Would you make your grandmother walk?"

Gloria sneered, "I can walk if it gets me away from these cretins," and grabbed the door handle.

Sam assisted, sliding the door to one side, and offering his arm to give his gran the extra support she needed.

"Don't you worry too much about me, Sam," she patted his arm with a spare hand. "I've barely had to walk anywhere today. I'm feeling rather sprightly. I'll be investing some of my pocket money in one of those scooters the first chance I get."

"There's an outlet on deck sixteen, Mrs Chalk," said Jermaine.

We walked away from the minibus and the Rio police without once looking back. They were not bad people, I knew that, but they had acted blindly and when the opportunity to take the easy route came along, they grabbed it with both hands.

The murder of Hector Benzali would be pinned on Sonia Noriega and that would be the end of it. She might even have done it; I genuinely hadn't figured that part out yet. Discovering Inigo Montoya ... sorry, Agent Patinkin was not part of the criminal organisation behind the treasure smuggling threw much of what I thought I knew into question. On the face of it, it seemed as though the police were not involved in a conspiracy to smuggle drugs and treasure. So what happened to the treasure in my safe? Who was the man who broke in last night? If the people in the backstreet industrial unit were FBI agents, then who sent the crew to attack us and who was the man who shot holes in their utility truck while we escaped in it?

Twenty-four hours into my investigation in Rio, I had more unknowns than I started with. It was irking me and though I knew gin wasn't much of a solution, it was currently the only one I could come up with.

I said goodbye to Gloria and Sam when we got inside the ship. Their cabin was on the crew decks; one fitted out to house a married couple but refurnished to fit two single beds instead. They had to travel down, I was travelling up.

Jermaine pushed the button for the top deck, and we rode in silence until he spoke just as the elevator car passed deck twelve.

"Madam, if there is anything I can do this evening to be of assistance ..."

I slid my arm through his, hooking my hand into his elbow as he crooked it and for a moment I rested my head against his muscular shoulder.

"Sweetie, what you should do is take the night off. We are due to sail before midnight and there is nothing I need you to do between now and tomorrow morning." I couldn't mention that I planned to have a bath because he would insist on running it if I did. I would eat with Alistair and tend to my own needs, perhaps relaxing with a book and spending time with my dachshunds – I had left them in the company of others too much the past two days.

Naturally, Jermaine resisted my suggestion, and I had to fight him. The man needed a life beyond looking after me. Don't get me wrong, I adored spending time with Jermaine and felt safer knowing he was close by, and it's not exactly a hardship to have a person who waits on me hand and foot. However, I also loved him enough to want him to have something in his life other than me.

The one thing I had done in the minibus heading back to the ship was text my friends. Barbie and Hideki had not returned to the ship just as I knew they wouldn't. Neither had Deepa and Martin, the two couples meeting up instead to find some food while they waited to hear from me.

Anders and Molly were the only ones who did make their way back to the Aurelia, though I had a fairly good idea why they wanted some time away from everyone else – young love is so ... physical.

Pushing that to one side, and trying very hard not to think about Finn Murphy, the treasure, Professor Noriega, and all the other elements of the mystery I was yet to solve, I swirled the water in my bath. Content it was the temperature I wanted, I returned to my bedroom where I left my clothes and removed my makeup. I was about to slip into the bath, an eBook device in my hands, when I reversed course and locked my door.

It might seem like overkill, but you would be surprised how often random people just wander into my suite. They are not always trying to kill me, and if they were a locked bedroom door was unlikely to prove much of a deterrent, but I hoped it might give me at least a few seconds of warning.

Slipping under the steaming surface of my extra-deep bath, I wriggled to get comfortable and focussed on the first page.

"Mrs Fisher!" Sam called my name while hammering on my bedroom door. I could hear him fruitlessly turning the handle. "Mrs Fisher!"

The dogs went nuts as usual, barking ferociously at the door and the people beyond it even though Sam was calling out to them as well.

"Calm down, girls. It's just Sam. You can be calm."

"Here let me try," Gloria insisted, rattling the door. "Maybe a run up is what I need," she remarked, powering me from the gloriously hot and delicately scented water with a vision of the mad old bat using whatever new mobility scooter she had bought herself as a battering r am.

"I'm coming!" I yelled.

"Ay?"

"Don't ram the door!

"Ay?" Either Gloria couldn't hear me or was pretending not to because she wanted to see what damage her scooter would do."

I'm coming!"

I heard Gloria comment to Sam, "Stand clear. I think she wants us to break it down."

Battling to get to the door while simultaneously fighting to wrap a towel around my sopping wet body, I caught my toes on the corner of the bed. Now hopping, swearing, and clutching my toes, Anna chose to add one more factor – avoiding a dancing, excited dog. It proved too much, and I fell, bumping my hip as I careened off my dressing table and back onto my bed.

Thinking I was in some distress, or perhaps being attacked by a randy sasquatch given some of the language I had chosen to employ, Gloria rammed the door anyway.

I managed to just about roll off the bed to snatch the sausage dogs out of the way before she ploughed into it with all the speed she could muster.

The handle popped off on my side, shooting across the room to smack into a wall and bounce off. The door itself flew open, whacking into the wall to leave a dent. It tried to rebound but found Gloria barrelling through the gap with Sam hard on her shoulder.

I was still only sort of wearing the towel, had a snarling dachshund under each arm, and parts of me on display that I really didn't want anyone but Alistair and a gynaecologist to see. Employing Anna and Georgie to cover my boobs, I instructed my 'guests' to get out.

If you are questioning whether I actually said, 'get out' then you are quite astute.

I did, however, follow my advice with a friendlier, "I will be out in a minute."

Sam, his face crimson, backed from the room with a hand over his eyes. Gloria cackled as she is wont to do, her scooter beeping as she reversed through my doorway once more.

Muttering ensued, but only for a moment, for a question stopped me.

"What drove you two to come looking for me in such a hurry?"

Gloria answered, "Sam figured it out."

Figured it out?

I was on my feet, inspecting my injured toes to see what damage I might have done. Surely, given the pain I was in, there had to be several of them with pieces of mangled bone sticking out. There wasn't. In fact, the only mark to suggest I had stubbed them at all was a slight scratch to the nail varnish on my big toe.

The girls had run off, leaving my bedroom to play with Sam now they had established it wasn't a mob of machine gun toting killers outside my bedroom door.

I wanted to get dressed, but the desire to know what Gloria was talking about drove me from my room with just the towel to cover myself. At least it was firmly held in place now.

Peeking around the doorframe, I asked, "Figured what out?"

Dinosaurs

Sam's goofy grin split his face when his gran aimed an arm his way and gave him the floor.

"It was plaster of Paris," he chuckled.

I didn't follow him. The question 'What was plaster of Paris?' forming in my head before I saw the answer for myself.

The white powder he found wasn't cocaine at all. At the time, I thought it looked or felt familiar but wasn't able to place it. Now that he had named it, I knew for certain he was correct.

"How did you figure that out?" I asked, wanting to hear his answer, but also trying to focus on the itch at the back of my skull the new information had just triggered.

"Lieutenant Jacobs has a cast on her arm," he grinned at me, pleased with himself. "I bumped into her in the passageway by our cabin."

"We were just going out to find some dinner," Gloria explained. "Sam saw the cast on her arm and knew immediately."

I nodded my head. The ship's medical centre, with limited facilities and space, used the old plaster of Paris casts rather than the new resin ones because they were cheaper and easier to stock.

Both Gloria and Sam were looking at me expectantly, waiting for me to say something, but my brain had shut out almost all other functions so it could focus on what this meant.

I had missed something vital. There was plaster of Paris on the floor in the room where Hector Benzali was packing Roman artefacts to send to America ... why? Sam said there was a large bag or bags of it. It didn't matter which it was for there was clearly a quantity of the substance and that required explanation.

My phone rang, invading my thoughts and bursting the chain of images I was working through as surely as a pin to a balloon.

It was on charge in my bedroom, buzzing away insistently.

Stalking back into my room to find it, I closed the door and fished out a pair of clean knickers after jabbing the green 'answer' button with a little more force than was necessary – I was giving up on my bath and I was feeling a tad aggravated about it.

"Hey, Patty," Barbie's Californian lilt filled my room. I knew it was her calling of course, and answered because it was the polite thing to do, but also because it was so unusual for her to phone me – texting is her thing, like most young people.

"It was plaster of Paris," I announced, only realising what a random comment it was after I had said it. "The white powder Sam found, I mean. It was plaster of Paris, not cocaine."

"Oh, right," she replied somewhat absentmindedly. "Did Schneider come back with you?"

I paused with my hand in my underwear drawer, rooting around for the bra that matched my panties.

Frowning, I said, "No. I thought he came back with you guys." I dredged my memory, trying to remember his last message, then picked up my phone, changing apps so I could see it.

I had told him the police might be in on the smuggling thing – which, of course, I now knew to be erroneous. He responded with '*Understood. I'll see you on the ship.*'

I relayed that to Barbie. "He was heading back here. I haven't seen him in hours. Is he not answering his phone?"

"No, Patty. Martin is getting worried. He checked with security at the doors, and he hasn't returned to the ship yet."

A heavy ball of worry formed in my gut. What did this mean? Three murders in short succession. They had to be connected. Three murders, treasure heading for the museum ... "Professor Geller," I murmured, my voice a whisper.

"What was that, Patty? I can hardly hear you."

Straining my brain to connect the dots, I spoke aloud. "I left Schneider with Professor Geller. The head of the museum had just been attacked – robbed and assaulted in the staff carpark when he arrived for work. Schneider took him to his office while we went to get the police. That was when we got chased."

"Ok, Patty. What about it? Where is he now?"

The itch at the back of my skull was driving me nuts. There was something I just wasn't seeing. Three murders. All along I'd been convinced all three were connected, but what if they were not? What if I was wrong about Professor Noriega being murdered? Or better yet, what if I was right but the murders were not connected after all.

The man who came to the ship pretending to be Professor Noriega hadn't killed Finn Murphy, I'd managed to figure that much out, but in so doing I assumed he was part of the smuggling ring at the museum. Of course, the concept of the smuggling ring only came to me when Hector was killed next to a bunch of packing crates.

What if this wasn't about the treasure and the two things weren't connected? It was one heck of a coincidence ...

"Patty!"

Barbie's yell jabbed my balloon of thought, bursting it just as the ringing phone had before.

This time, though, I didn't lose track of what I was thinking, and said, "How soon can you get to my cabin?"

The answer to that one turned out to be less than five minutes because she was already on route. Hideki was with her as were the remaining four members of my security team.

Hurrying, I finished getting dressed, opting for running shoes, stretchy jeans, and a super casual hoody because it went with the ballcap I stuffed my hair into since there was no time to dry or style it.

As I performed those tasks, I forced my mind to be calm. The information I needed was in there. I had seen it at some point. Viewing the case from a completely new angle, one where the treasure had no connection to what happened to Hector, and discounting the possibility that Sonia Noriega had killed him, I was left with very little to go on.

It all came back to the packing room where Hector died. There was plaster of Paris on the floor. Hector Benzali was packing Roman artefacts to send to America ...

I picked up my phone to check something, a niggle in a far corner of my brain certain it had just glimpsed the truth.

The answer hit me like a sucker punch to the stomach and I gasped aloud.

The polite yet urgent knock at my door occurred less than a second later.

"Madam?"

"I thought I told you to take the night off?"

"Yes, madam. However, I heard of Lieutenant Schneider's plight and anticipated another trip into Rio."

Gloria said, just as I was entering the suite's main living space, "I thought that police captain said he would arrest you if you went ashore again?"

"That's a risk we are just going to have to take."

Martin, Deepa, Molly, Barbie, and everyone else were in my suite and looking my way. I had their full attention, so I said the word none of them were expecting to hear.

"Dinosaurs."

You could have dropped a pin.

Seconds passed, broken by Barbie when she repeated, "Dinosaurs?"

I pulled up the zip on my hoody. "Yup. Let's go."

I was heading for the door and leaving them all behind me. They couldn't see it, but I had a smirk on my face.

Cries of 'Patty!' and 'Mrs Fisher!' followed me though I refused to break my stride. They wanted to know what the heck I was talking about. Treasure and how everything was to do with it had been the only concept leaving my lips since we arrived in Brazil. Dropping the word 'Dinosaur' and walking out was like rolling a grenade into the midst of everything they understood.

They wanted to know more, naturally, but I couldn't fill in the blanks because I wasn't sure I understood them myself.

Jermaine caught up to me first, falling into step by my side. Always ready to support whatever madcap scheme I might devise without feeling any need to question it, he said nothing and kept pace.

The next to arrive were Anna and Georgie.

I said, "Ah."

"Shall I return them to your cabin, madam?"

The girls were happily prancing along next to me, one on either side of my feet. They were vaccinated and had their pet's passports. It didn't get them into every country, but Brazil was one they could enter without the need for quarantine.

Despite that fact, it wasn't like I was heading out for a nice evening stroll.

Huffing out a disappointed breath, I crouched to scoop them both, kissing their heads before handing them to Jermaine who would return them to my suite.

"Mummy will be back soon, girls," I promised, praying it would prove to be true. The ship was due to sail soon.

Wheeling her wheelchair faster than was advisable in the tight passageway, and with Gloria right on her backside astride the scooter of mayhem – purple, just like the one she hired – Barbie demanded to know what was going on.

"Patricia Fisher, you tell me what any of this has to do with dinosaurs right now!"

We turned the corner into a wide space that looked down over the central entertainment area of the ship. To our right was a bank of elevators and passengers were just exiting one of them.

Jermaine darted forward to stop the doors from closing and I walked backward behind him talking to Barbie. This slowed her down, so Gloria and Sam went around her.

"Did I say dinosaurs? Sorry, I meant fossils." I backed into the elevator car just as the doors swished shut, cutting off her expletive laden cry of disbelief.

Travelling down through the ship, Jermaine said, "There will be no limousines, madam. Not at this time of the day. We are due to sail in less than four hours."

I nodded my understanding. "Then we had better hope we can find a taxi."

It transpired that Jermaine was wrong or, at least, sort of. The cruise line's official limousines, there to take their top-flight guests wherever they wanted to go, had packed in for the night, but we stepped out of the ship just as two were pulling up to return their passengers.

John Oswald, an American billionaire in his eighties, and his twen-ty-something fiancé from England, Betty Ross, exited the rearmost limo.

"Mrs Fisher!" hallooed John, waving cheerfully. He was holding Betty's hand and looking very much the man in love. Betty did too and despite their rather large age gap, and her humble background, I got no hint that she was in it for his money. "Is Mrs Philips still due to join us in Miami?"

"Indeed she is," I beamed at them both. My old friend Felicity Philips was flying out to meet the ship at its next port of call. From there, she and her assistant, Mindy, would travel with us to New York where the wedding would take place. Many of the wedding guests were also boarding in Miami, taking full advantage of the opportunity for a two-day party. The guest list read like a who's who of modern-day celebrities. I knew Alistair was pleased – it would get the ship a lot of exposure, but I could not help but feel it would all just be a lot of unnecessary noise.

"Are you heading into town?" asked Betty. "Aren't we sailing soon?"

"We are," I nodded. "I've just got a couple of errands to run first."

Barbie exited the ship at that point, arriving a minute after me due to the elevators.

"There she is," she yelled in faux anger. "Someone grab Patty so I can run over her foot. That will slow her down."

John Oswald's eyes flared. "Everything all right, Patricia?"

A sigh puffed out my cheeks, but I nodded. "Yes. Sorry, you'll have to excuse us. We have a really small window to get stuff done."

The chauffeur advised that he was expected to return to the depot now, though he changed his mind the moment Jermaine produced a wad of cash. The second limo was similarly commandeered, sweeping majestically out of the port and into Rio once more.

The sun had set, giving the city a very different look as we cruised past a piece of beach. There were people partying on the sand, the many bars and open-air clubs filled with locals and tourists alike all revelling in the warmth of the evening.

I twisted in my seat to wave at Barbie in the second limo and got a rude gesture in reply. It made me snigger. Of all my friends, she was always the one who wanted to know not only what I had figured out but how. It drove her nuts that I would never reveal my inner thoughts until the time was right.

"Madam," Jermaine interrupted my thoughts. "The museum will be closed now, will it not?"

I nodded. "I certainly hope so."

Eyeing me sceptically, he relaxed back into his seat.

I had Sam and Gloria in the limo too, my assistant idly spinning his magnifying glass between thumb and forefinger of his right hand. Gloria watched the city go by outside her window, keeping her own thoughts.

Her scooter was one that could be folded down and split into pieces. Each piece was then easy to load into a boot and none were so heavy that an older person, weakened with age, would struggle to lift or manoeuvre them.

At the Museum of Brazil, visiting for the third time in two days, I had the driver stop short.

"Can you wait for us?" I enquired.

He sucked on his teeth. He'd probably had a long day and fancied getting home to put his feet up. Or take a bath, I remembered my own attempt at bathing. However, we were down to three and a half hours now and missing the sailing time would not go down well.

I held up a bunch of twenty-dollar bills, fanning them out and watching his eyes count them greedily.

"Two hours" I told him. "If we are not out in two hours, feel free to go. Your friend in the other limo gets the same if he waits. We need a reliable ride to get back to the ship."

The driver licked his lips and nodded: he would wait.

On the pavement a moment later and with Gloria's mobility scooter reassembled and all my friends raring to go, I accepted that I needed to tell them something.

"This was never about treasure," I explained, pointing my feet toward the entrance to the museum's staff carpark.

Martin shook his head in confusion.

"But someone broke into your suite last night to steal what we found on board the ship."

"That's separate," I replied. "It has to be. Nothing else makes sense."

He accepted my reply as gospel and said, "Okay. I guess I don't care too much what crime is at the centre of this. I'm here to get Schneider back. How sure are you that he is here?"

I had to grit my teeth at this point. There was no way to hide that I just didn't know if he was here or not. Going with the truth, I admitted, "I'm not."

Lieutenant Commander Martin Baker's eyes popped out on stalks.

"But we don't know where he is, and Professor Geller does. He's behind it all and he's here right now."

Barbie had a hard time with that one.

"Professor Geller?"

"Yes."

"The head of the museum?"

"Yes."

"The dusty, old dinosaur bone expert we met earlier?"

"Yes." Goodness this was taking too long. I chose to take a short cut. "I'm sorry it took me so long to figure it out, but here it is in the shortest version I can give you. Fossils are worth a fortune. Like millions.

Not just any old fossil you can pick up off the beach, obviously, but I looked up a few that had sold on the open market earlier. A tooth from a T-Rex went for $18000.00. That's just one tooth. How many teeth are in a T-Rex's head?"

No one knew the answer, but they didn't need to because the point was made, and Barbie could see it. "Professor Geller said there were so many fossils being found now they had to hire extra people to catalogue them and had a backlog that was going to take more than a year to get through."

I picked up what she was saying, "Exactly. No one will miss the ones he takes and sells off, especially since they are yet to be catalogued. He's shipping them to a partner in the Smithsonian, sending them to a lucrative, rich US market without having to pay any customs duty and he's doing it undetected by hiding them inside artefacts that are genuinely being shipped between the museums."

"The Roman jugs and bowls," said Jermaine, cottoning on.

"That they are filling with ..." I pointed my finger at Sam.

"Plaster of Paris!" he trumpeted triumphantly.

"Exactly. When we were looking at the scene around where Hector was killed, there was a fossil on the table – a raptor claw or something like that."

Barbie held up her arms to stop me.

"Okay, Patty. Let's say you have all that right. What makes you think Professor Geller is in there right now holding Schneider hostage and prime for us to catch in the act?"

It was a good question and one I had been expecting. We'd been talking for the last two minutes though, and time was not on our side.

'I'll tell you after you have sweet talked the guard into opening the gate."

Barbie blinked at me, running my request through her head before saying, "I'm in a wheelchair, Patty."

"And?"

Jermaine joined in. "Yes, Barbie, and? You think people in wheelchairs are instantly unattractive?"

The heat rising off her cheeks came instantly.

"No, of course not!" she blurted, horrified that anyone might believe that of her. "I was just saying that ..."

Deepa stopped her. "Girl, you are drop dead gorgeous in or out of a wheelchair. Go charm the guard, will you?"

Still embarrassed, Barbie spoke quietly when she said, "I'm not prettier than you, Deepa. You could charm the guard."

It drew a chuckle from her friend. "Yeah, but I'm married now, and I give off a married vibe that men seem to pick up on. I flirt with them, but they know. It's like they can smell the ring."

"That's right," agreed her husband, nodding his head then stopping abruptly. "What do you mean by 'you flirt with them?'"

Deepa rolled her eyes and made shooing motions.

Barbie huffed a breath that ruffled her lips, undid two buttons on her top and started to wheel herself toward the gate, muttering the whole way.

We were just out of sight of the staff entrance. The pedestrian gate was right by the vehicle entrance, and it didn't matter which one she got open, we just needed to get inside. This part of my plan was a little ... naughty. That was the best word I could come up with. The most innocent sounding anyway.

The guard on the gate would alert the guards inside if he got the chance. Barbie had to distract him in such a way that he would open the gate to let her in. Then we would rush in and overpower the poor fellow.

Naughty. But necessary. And justified in the long run. To bring down a smuggling ring that was prepared to murder a person, I would tie someone up for an hour and not feel too bad about it. Heck, maybe he was in on it anyway.

More time than I expected Barbie to need ticked by and just when I was about to ask Hideki – the one peering around the corner to watch her – he announced that she was on her way back.

"Huh? She failed?" Honestly, that eventuality had never once entered my mind. We needed to get by the guard, and she was my way in.

Barbie's smile always worked. It lit up a room like a firework in a jar and her gravity-defying boobs did the rest. Men were powerless.

She wheeled back into sight and around the corner.

"Jermaine, you're up," she sniggered.

Failing to follow what she was saying, I looked at Jermaine.

"The gentleman in question prefers men," he explained.

"Oh," I made an 'oops' face at Barbie and did my best to resist urging Jermaine to work fast.

"You're sure he's gay?" I asked Barbie.

She chuckled again. "When a man never once tries to look down my top, it's a fairly good indicator."

A few seconds later a resounding clang echoed into the night. It came from the direction of the gate and caused the lot of us to rush to the corner and peek out.

Jermaine had one hand through the bars of the gate where it held the guard by the front of his uniform. He'd reached in, grabbed him, and gave a yank. The guard's head had hit the steel bars and he was out cold.

Jermaine lowered him carefully to the floor and fished around in his trouser pockets until he produced a set of keys. On it was a little electronic doodad which operated the gate mechanism when he got it close to the control panel.

We were in!

The Man Behind It All

As one we surged forward, hurrying to get through the gate. The first ones there – Hideki and Martin, helped Jermaine hoist the dead weight of the unconscious guard from the ground. Carrying him out of sight and into the shadows to the side of his little guard hut, they placed him back down.

"One of you needs to wear his clothes," I pointed out.

Martin understood why. "We have no idea when they will change the guard, so we have to be prepared for someone to turn up before this is over."

"And we cannot afford for them to sound the alarm until we are ready," I added, looking squarely at Hideki.

"Me?" he questioned.

Jermaine pointed out a key factor. "You are the only one who will fit into this guy's clothes."

It was true. The chap was about Hideki's size, which is roughly five feet nine inches tall and slender. Standing six feet four inches and most of a hundred pounds heavier, Jermaine wouldn't even get his legs into the guard's trousers. Baker was shorter, but too broad. Sam was shorter still, but again too broad across the shoulders.

"What about Anders?" Hideki identified the other member of the team who was small enough to wear the guard's clothes.

Jermaine and Martin pulled Hideki into a quick huddle, undoubtedly pointing out that when the next guard came, he would need to be restrained and we all knew Hideki was capable of doing precisely that. He was small, but so was Bruce Lee and they had about the same level of fighting prowess. Anders was small and would get his teeth pushed in

.

I had another reason for wanting it to be Hideki. "It's best if it's you because I need Barbie to stay out here too." I had to twist around to find her squinting at me with accusing eyes.

"It's because of the wheelchair, isn't it?" She was not pleased about being discounted from the team.

"Well, no, actually. I have something else I need you to do when the rest of us go inside. However, we may have to move fast in there – I have no idea what we are going to find, and the building is set over several floors including a basement."

Gloria cleared her throat in an overly loud fashion.

"I suppose that means you plan to leave me outside too then."

"I'm sorry, Gloria. Truly I am. The rest of the team are trained security officers. Or in Jermaine's case, a stunt double for Batman." My joke brought some well-timed laughter when we were all feeling nervous. "We won't have time to wait for you. Stay here and help Barbie."

"What's blondie going to be doing then?" Gloria asked grumpily.

Barbie jinked her eyebrows at me to reiterate Gloria's question.

I told her.

She laughed. "Easy stuff then. I'll get to it."

The guys stripped off the guard, who started to come around while they were removing his clothes. A handy roll of duct tape they found in the guard hut soon dealt with his hands and feet and provided a neat gag to the soundtrack of profuse apologies. They placed him inside the hut where he would be warmer, and we all hoped it wouldn't be long before we got to free him.

Just before we set off, I did three things. First, I walked a few paces away from the guard hut, made sure the bound and gagged guard was in the frame and took a selfie. I got a few questioning looks from my friends which I chose to ignore. Secondly, I checked my watch, performed some mental calculations, gave up because I was just guessing how long it would take, and sent it to someone I knew would be ... *excited* to receive it. Thirdly, I hooked the key out of Gloria's scooter.

"Hey!" she swiped at my arm to get it back, narrowly missing and firing off a torrent of curse words when I skipped out of reach.

"It's for your own good," I sang, pocketing the key. There wasn't a chance in hell Gloria would have stayed where she was. The moment we were out of sight, she would have been after us.

Leaving Barbie with Hideki and Gloria, I followed my security team around the back of the museum. Getting into the building was another tricky bit, but one I felt more confident about than the front gate.

We passed the guardroom earlier today while running away from Bruno and Jordana, so I knew they had a fire extinguisher as a doorstop and their door was open just as I hoped it would be.

Crouching low to stay out of sight as we approached, we could all see where there were lights shining up from a pair of basement windows set into the ground. A whispered message passed down our snaking line – that was our target, that was where we were heading.

The only light on in the whole building was the guardroom. Lights coming from two windows in the basement had to be Professor Geller and whoever was with him.

We stayed quiet as mice as we scrambled under the guardroom window - not that there was much chance of the guards hearing us or even seeing us if we had chosen to stroll by at normal height. They had their TV turned up and were watching a soccer game with enthusiasm.

Once inside and a corridor over from the guards, I allowed myself to breathe a sigh of relief. So far so good, and we even believed we knew where we needed to go.

Looking for a set of stairs to lead us down and navigating in the dark passages by the use of the light from a single phone, it took us a while to find a door labelled 'subsolo' which Martin assured me meant basement.

Gripping the handle, Martin tried to turn it one way, then the other.

"It's locked," he muttered.

"I can pick that," volunteered Molly, scurrying forward. She caught my eye as she passed. "What, Mrs Fisher? I'm from the rough end of Maidstone. I was breaking into places before I was ten." I watched her pull her hair into a ponytail, rolling a hairband off her wrist to hold it in place. Hair out of the way, she produced a tiny tool roll from a back pocket.

The matter settled, Martin held the light for her so she could see to work and asked me, "How is it that you knew there would be people here tonight? You seem certain Professor Geller has Schneider held captive and that he himself is here now."

We couldn't advance and everyone was looking inward for me to explain.

"He got beaten up in a brazen attack on museum grounds. He then claimed it was a young man who attacked him and said he was robbed. Only thing is, he was wearing a Patek Philippe watch."

Jermaine emitted a low whistle.

Molly stopped what she was doing to ask, "What's the big deal about a watch? Are they expensive?"

Deepa said, "And then some."

I continued to explain, "I don't think they took his wallet either – there was a bulge in his jacket right where it would be, and an opportunistic thief probably would have taken his car – a new Aston Martin."

Deepa interrupted. "Okay, so if he wasn't robbed, what did happen?"

I gave her the short but cryptic answer. "He got a reminder." Seeing the dimly lit bewildered faces staring back at me, I helped them out. "Professor Geller is a dinosaur expert – a palaeontologist. He knows fossils inside out. Maybe the smuggling thing was his idea and maybe it was someone else's, but he willingly gets himself involved and leverages his position to make people at the museum help him."

"How exactly does that lead to him getting beaten up today?" asked Anders, his voice echoing what everyone else wanted to know.

"I'm getting to that part. When I spoke to Professor Baccarin yesterday, he expressed sorrow for his former colleague Professor Noriega who never got to achieve his one goal in life." I paused for dramatic effect. "To be granted tenure here. As a professor, getting tenure is everything. I think Geller coerced Sonia Noriega into smuggling the dinosaur fossils out of the museum by holding her father's dream over her head." I could see no one was able to follow my logic. "Noriega dying destabilised Geller's machine. With her father dead, Geller no longer held sway over Sonia."

"But surely she is too far in by now?" questioned Deepa. "She couldn't go to the police, not without being considered complicit."

"Yes, and it's worse than that. Let's circle back to Professor Geller getting beaten up today. Money is changing hands across borders and people are getting quietly rich through a highly illegal criminal enterprise."

Martin was the first to put it together. "Someone found out."

"That's my guess," I nodded my head in the dark. "It could have started in America, but whatever the case, Professor Geller got a visit from someone far more dangerous and willing to do violence than he was used to and what was he supposed to do? It wasn't like he could call the cops either. My guess is that he was being leaned on."

"That's what organised criminals do," muttered Deepa. "They start taking and then they never stop, increasing their demands until they have everything, and you survive only to feed them."

"When Sonia bailed on Geller, refusing to be a part of his little smuggling ring any longer, it meant the product was no longer being moved. Geller's bosses tolerated it for a while, but eleven days on from Professor Noriega being killed, they decided to give Professor Geller an unfriendly reminder."

"The beating in the carpark," said Sam, proving he was able to follow the story.

I touched his hand. "That's right, sweetie. I'm guessing, but I suspect that Professor Geller murdered Hector Benzali when he found him in the packing room upstairs. No one else was supposed to know, and I am further guessing that Sonia told him about it. They were heard arguing in the days leading up to his death. I believe they were arguing about her decision to refuse to play along. Perhaps Hector understood the ramifications and was trying to fill in for her. I could have that part completely wrong. We'll know soon enough."

"Got it!" cheered Molly, doing so without raising her voice.

The lock turned and the door swung outward toward us. Nothing but silence beckoned in the darkness beyond. No one spoke; there was no need for any words. If Schneider was down there, we would get him back. If he wasn't, we would get answers.

Simple Tasks

Outside at the guard hut, Barbie was talking on the phone. The simple task Patricia gave her was ever so easy: just track down the FBI detachment deployed here to find the smuggling ring and get hold of Agent Patinkin. Oh, and do it without talking to the police or telling the FBI who you are.

Easy.

The FBI would be tracing her call, Barbie was sure of that, but had wisely used the guard's so they wouldn't have her number when this was over.

The task turned out to be easier than she imagined it could be. Not that she had managed to get through to Agent Patinkin yet, but she had been able to call the FBI in Langley, speak to a person at their switchboard, and get her call rerouted to the local office here in Rio.

Not knowing a huge amount about law enforcement, it had surprised Barbie to learn that the FBI had offices outside of the United States. Until tonight, she thought they dealt with domestic cases only, but it turned out the Bureau had detachments all over the world where they could intervene and investigate on behalf of US citizens in those locations.

Idly scratching at an itch on her arm, Barbie twisted in her wheelchair to stretch her back and had to fight to stifle a yawn that split her face.

Shooting a tired smile at her boyfriend and thinking to herself that he looked good in uniform, even if it was that of a museum night guard, she spotted, or rather didn't spot, something that should have been there.

Sitting up straight in her chair as she waited for her call to be taken off hold, she asked, "Where's Gloria?"

The Raid

Walking silently, Martin, Jermaine and all the others forged ahead of me, which is to say they made me go last. They were my security team, and we had no idea what we were about to walk into.

In all likelihood, it would be Professor Geller and an assistant. I believed the smuggling of valuable dinosaur fossils was a small operation, not one that required a team of people.

The only part that worried me was Schneider's continued absence. He was a big man and well trained too. Ordinarily, there would be nothing a man the size and age of Professor Geller could do to get the upper hand. I couldn't even picture the head of the museum getting away with pulling a gun – Schneider would swat it from his hand at the first opportunity.

A stun gun though, a taser, the offer of a drink he had quickly laced with a drug ... all these things were designed to even the playing field. If that wasn't the case, then Professor Geller had help and I didn't like that idea at all.

The team knew my speculations; not that it made any difference to their plans – they came ashore with Schneider, and they were going to go back to the ship with him or not at all.

The lights in the basement were on, a small mercy that meant we would not be blinded by the glare when we burst into a brightly lit room. Unfortunately, it also meant we didn't know which door we wanted. Had the corridors been dark, we would have been able to see light spilling from under the door frame or around the sides.

Instead, we had to rely on the passage of sound and stay extra quiet so we could hear the murmur of voices muffled by the thick doors of the old building. There was nothing. No sound.

Until we heard Schneider, that is.

Pushing me to the side – they didn't want me to be part of the raiding party – my friends lined up on either side of the door. Martin and Deepa were at the front, Jermaine and Anders were right on their shoulders with Molly and Sam poised to follow.

Martin held up three fingers, silently mouthing his countdown as he folded his fingers inward.

My heart beat like mad in my chest and I fingered the phone in my pocket. Was it time to send the text? I wanted to. It would signal the end of this adventure and with time dwindling, I was going to have to send it soon whether I wanted to or not. I held off though, waiting to see what was behind the door and questioned, for the millionth time, why the crimes I solved so often ended like this.

Why did it have to be a rescue at night in an old building? Why couldn't I solve mysteries like Miss Marple did? Calmly and with a dignified air. I read Agatha Christie's books as a child and was certain the sleuths never ran screaming from crazed gunmen in any of her stories.

It felt like I did that all the time.

Martin's last finger folded down and he exploded into motion. Shoulder barging his way through the door even as he turned the handle, the team of six burst into the room yelling orders to cause confusion and fanning out instantly so they weren't a big target.

The loose plan, because they had no idea what sights might greet them on the other side of the door, was to go in hard and act like they were armed police officers. Barking orders to scare the room's occupants was a tactic fraught with danger though. What if Professor Geller was armed? What if he had friends with him? What if his friends were less than friendly *and* armed?

The yelling lasted about a second, petering out as one by one my team came to realise there was no one to yell at.

I peered around the corner.

Professor Geller wasn't in the room, and neither was Schneider despite the fact that we could hear him.

His voice was coming from a speaker mounted on a desk.

Sam asked, "What's going on, Mrs Fisher?"

Less than five seconds had passed since they ran through the door; enough time for the truth of our situation to dawn on everyone.

Twisting to face the door where I was still standing, Martin's eyes were wide and filled with fear.

He yelled the words burning into the front of my brain, "It's a trap!"

Everyone was moving, heading back toward me where I stood frozen in the exit. They didn't move far though. They took one step each and froze just like me.

I knew why. A shadow had fallen across me. In the space between seeing it and taking my next breath, the unforgiving steel muzzle of a gun pressed into my side.

"Good evening, Mrs Fisher and friends," said Professor Geller with genuine warmth. "You are delightfully predictable."

Gloria

Elsewhere in the museum, Gloria was completely lost. Bored of hanging around outside, and curious to see what fun Patricia and all the others were getting up to, she had waited until neither Dr Hideki, as she referred to him, nor Barbie the blonde bombshell were looking her way.

The moment their backs were turned, she took the spare key from her pocket, inserted it into the scooter's ignition, and grinned wildly as her transport silently trundled away.

Of course, she had no idea where Patricia had gone, only that they were heading into the museum's back rooms where the public would never usually venture.

Convinced she could find her way around – she'd been in there just a few hours ago after all – Gloria soon discovered the building was significantly more vast than she remembered.

Nothing struck her as familiar, her hope to find a display piece to use as a reference point never coming.

By and by, she found herself in a large hallway lined along one side with suits of armour.

The Double Bluff

"Please join your friends, Mrs Fisher," Professor Geller requested in his polite Brazilian accented tone. There was no danger, however, that I could misconstrue it as a polite request for he jammed the gun into my ribs with the intent to bruise.

Seeing me wince, Jermaine's top lip curled though he remained where he was, watching for now.

Behind Professor Geller came four more men, three of whom held handguns. They trained them on my friends, forcing the whole team to back away with their hands up.

The fourth man wore a suit, much like Professor Geller but his was smarter, more expensive, and fit him a lot better. He was also thirty years Professor Geller's junior and looked like an artist's impression of a gang boss. He had no neck; his head simply tiered into his shoulders. There were tattoos on the skin between his chin and his collar and more poking out the cuffs of his black shirt. His hair was buzzcut and he exuded the attitude of a person who would kill as a convenient solution.

Darting ahead to join my friends, I spun around to find the head of the museum smirking at me.

"Predictable," he grinned, repeating a word that stung. I had walked us right into a trap. How had he known what I would do?

"Let me guess," he said, "You convinced yourself that I was being forced to participate in the fossil smuggling operation, yes?"

I didn't answer.

"You saw my attack earlier and probably noticed that I hadn't actually been robbed."

I couldn't stop my face from twitching, my eyes flaring slightly when he admitted it was staged and he saw my reaction.

It made him smile.

Turning his head slightly to the left without actually taking his eyes off me, he spoke to the man in the suit. "I told you she would fall for it, Carlos."

Carlos just looked bored. "Very good, Lino. However, you are yet to explain why you felt the need to set such an intricate trap. We now have a whole bunch of bodies to dispose of, so you will find me less than thankful for the extra work."

Professor Geller gave a slight shake of his head, dismayed at his partner's lack of vision.

"But don't you see? This is the woman who took down the Alliance of Families. The moment she contacted the museum to request a meeting with Professor Noriega's colleagues, I knew she would sniff out our little smuggling enterprise. By feeding her juicy little breadcrumbs of information and showing just what I wanted her to see, I manipulated the conclusion she would draw. It wasn't easy, you know." Professor Geller frowned for the first time, disappointed by how unimpressed people were by his genius.

"You were never the pawn," I concluded. "You are the mastermind."

"Precisely," Geller grinned. "I have two ex-wives that are rinsing me for every Real I have ever earned. I needed a source of income they couldn't touch, and the museum has so much valuable inventory a man with a few friends in low places can sell."

The 'low places' remark made Carlos cut his eyes at the professor.

"There were never supposed to be any deaths," growled Carlos.

Professor Geller frowned at him, "Oh, come along now, Carlos, you can't tell me Hector's murder bothers you."

"Bodies draw attention," Carlos growled. "One was bad enough. Now you hand me this lot and expect me to deal with them?"

Geller's upbeat attitude faltered, turning dark.

"That's your end of the business, Carlos. I provide the means and the product. You ensure things run smoothly both here and in the States. You iron out the problems."

Carlos raised his voice to reply, "This is a problem of your making!"

"No, Carlos, this is a solution I have provided to a problem that dropped unexpectedly into my lap!" As if embarrassed at having raised his voice, the professor looked away and used his left hand to sweep his blazing red hair back across his forehead as he composed himself.

I needed time. *We* needed time. The text message I sent earlier was going to save us, but not if they shot us first.

"Who killed Hector?" I asked.

Professor Geller positively beamed with joy.

"You really don't know, do you?" the man revelled in his own genius. "I must say I rather enjoyed pitching myself against a worthy adversary. Even if, in the end, you proved to be no match at all."

"So it was you," I nodded my head. "He wasn't part of the plan, was he? You expected to find Sonia hard at work, but discovered her boyfriend instead."

Now the professor looked irritated. "Yes, yes. Well, done, Mrs Fisher, you figured something out for yourself. Sonia refused to continue the work after her father died. She said I no longer held any sway over her. I threatened to kill her if she didn't comply. That was why I had the gun with me, you see? It was her own fault really."

That I had figured part of the mystery out for myself was of little comfort. I had been played, my ego allowing me to follow Professor Geller's false trail of clues and here we were.

Or were we?

There were a couple of things I hadn't told anyone. The first was the phone call I got just before my team rushed into the basement. I'd known it was coming ... no, I suppose that's not quite accurate. I'd chosen to convince myself it was coming. Barbie had never let me down before, so when my phone – switched to silent, obviously – started to vibrate against my right bum cheek just before I followed everyone into Professor Geller's trap, I whispered quietly to the person at the other end and put it back in my pocket.

The other thing I omitted to tell my team was to do with the selfie I took. I was still waiting for that one to pan out and could feel a few tendrils of doubt squirming around in my belly. The selfie was belt *and* braces though, a backup just in case Barbie couldn't get through to the FBI agents here in Rio.

A smile tugged at one corner of my mouth. It did not go unmissed by the five men facing me.

Slowly, I lowered my right hand, turning my hips a little so they could see I was reaching for the phone in my back pocket.

Carefully extracting it, I turned the device so they could see the screen.

"You idiot!" raged Carlos. "She's just captured every word you've said!"

The guns all twitched, the gunmen picking targets instead of just aiming in our general direction.

Speaking quickly, I squealed, "If you shoot us, there will be no chance you can get away with it."

Professor Geller, his face blotchy with rage, stormed across the room to snatch the phone from my hand.

"Who is this?" he demanded to know.

"This is Agent Patinkin of the FBI. You may know me better as Inigo Montoya, Professor Baccarin's grad student from California. Police are on their way to the museum now. Please stay where you are."

Geller thumbed the red button to end the call, his eyes focused on the device in his hand and his mouth shut.

I figured it was touch and go whether they would choose to obey or not. To be clear, this was never my plan. I hoped to find Professor Geller packing dinosaur fossils himself or with a helper, coerced or otherwise. His ploy to lure me into believing he was a victim worked completely, I won't hide that from you.

Asking Barbie to track down the FBI agent and have him call my phone was precautionary only. That the call came in just before we ran into a trap was nothing short of serendipity working in my favour for once.

The good news was that the bad guys were caught. Professor Geller and Carlos were on record confessing to the smuggling ring and to killing Hector, a crime which would see the professor behind bars for the rest of his life.

Geller launched the phone at the wall, destroying it. "Very clever, Mrs Fisher. Enjoy your victory, it will be short lived."

"Boss?" One of the gunmen glanced over his shoulder, a nervousness to his eyes now. "Don't you think we ought to get out of here?"

"Yeah," agreed the next gunman in line. "This place is gonna be crawling with cops soon. They don't got my voice on record. I didn't confess to anything."

The professor's partner in crime agreed with the principle of leaving. He didn't need to say it, I could see it in his face. He was about to bolt.

Sensing his enterprise failing, Professor Geller raised his gun again, pointing it right at me.

I squealed, "Jermaine!" Reacting automatically, my eyes scrunched shut, but I heard the bark of a a gun when it went off and I flinched.

I opened my eyes again a moment later. Not because I wasn't hurt, which I wasn't, but due to the fact that a curse-filled scream had accompanied the shot and a scuffle was now taking place.

My eyelids snapped open to a scene of utter bedlam.

In the doorway behind Professor Geller and the thugs, Sonia Noriega was having a gun ripped from her hands by Carlos. The shot had come from her, not the professor, and it had hit the man responsible for her boyfriend's murder.

Geller had a wound in his left shoulder and pain etched into his features.

The three gunmen, having already decided running away to fight another day was the policy they should follow, had been twitching toward the door when Sonia fired off her shot.

Now the three of them were being set upon by my entire team of security officers.

I got all that in the space between heartbeats, my feet frozen to the floor despite urgent messages from my brain to get them moving.

Carlos threw the much lighter Sonia to one side, taking her gun with him as he fled the room. She crunched into the opposite wall, striking her head to then fall unconscious to the floor in the corridor. Professor Geller, blood leaking from both sides of his jacket, stumbled out after Carlos, propelled by one of the henchmen who probably believed saving the professor would help his own cause.

The confines of the small basement room and the number of limbs getting thrown around prevented anyone from landing a telling blow. My own people were getting in each other's way as all six tried to eliminate the threat posed by the two remaining gunmen.

They were disarmed swiftly, but put up a strong fight, proving their worth as henchmen, I guess, while also delaying any of us from following their boss.

How far could the professor and Carlos get in five seconds? To the stairs and out of the basement probably and they had at least that much head start on us.

With the door forming a natural bottleneck and the two thugs pressed hard against it, no one could get out.

Where the heck were the cops? I sent the selfie I took to Captain Santoro with a simple message – '*Come get me, copper!*' It was a little on the nose, but the man threatened to throw me in jail if I set foot back on Rio soil and I believed a picture of me would get him moving far faster than a long message explaining Professor Geller was really behind it all. Captain Santoro had made it quite clear he wasn't inclined to believe anything I said.

Jermaine swung a punch over the top of everyone else, the blow blocked by the intended target though his defensive posture allowed Deepa to deliver a kick to the man's midsection.

He didn't go down and it was all taking far too long. The lead afforded to Carlos and the professor was coming up on ten seconds.

With a sigh, I looked around until I spotted what I wanted. Finding one of the thugs' pistols poking out from under the edge of a bench, I pointed it toward the ceiling and pulled the trigger. I tried to do it without flinching, but failed to pull that off.

I flinched again when a load of plaster rained down onto my head like hailstones made from ball bearings.

There followed a split second where everyone paused to look my way. Then, because the henchmen's attention was no longer on defending themselves, a flurry of limbs took them both out.

Deepa burst from the room, leading the pack by running over the fallen gunmen. Molly careened out after her with Sam and Martin right on her heels.

Anders, however, reversed course, nodded his thanks to me and took the gun I now held daintily from the tips of my thumb and forefinger like it was something distasteful I'd inadvertently picked up.

Jermaine found the other weapon, but instead of racing after the team who we could hear thundering down the corridor outside, he offered me his elbow.

"Shall we, madam?"

I slapped his arm and took off, yelling over my shoulder. "Run, you big dummy! And bring Sonia with you!"

Knight on a Steed

I got into the corridor in time to see Martin vanish around the corner. He was climbing the stairs, the sound of three more sets of feet hammering on the stone ahead of him.

I heard shouts of, "Which way?" from Deepa and footsteps again when they set off once more.

We were running again; another thing I could not recall Miss Marple ever having to do in her stories. I ran from or toward danger with such regularity that I knew to choose running shoes before we left the ship tonight.

Out of breath by the time we reached the top of the stairs, I only paused because I hadn't seen which way my friends went.

I wasn't chasing Carlos and the professor; my effort was solely so I was there when my team caught up to them. The police were coming, I was certain of that, but most of my team were not known to Captain Santoro and I didn't want anyone getting accidentally shot by the police.

Reaching an intersection, I could hear running feet, but the high ceilings, and labyrinthian nature of the building made the direction we needed hard to pinpoint.

Until I heard a banshee war cry that would stay with me until my dying day.

That it was Gloria's voice echoing through the halls was never in question. What she was doing, though, I felt an urgent need to know.

Her scream of terror-inducing rage ended in a string of swearwords a soldier would be proud to recite. A startled cry of horror with a deep Brazilian accent sounded in response, followed by a cry of pain followed swiftly by another and then another.

Cursing in Portuguese erupted, but it didn't last long and the abruptness with which it was silenced made me double my pace.

What had Gloria done?

Running so fast I could only make a right turn by bouncing off the wall with my shoulder, I came into a new hallway to find the view blocked by Deepa, Martin, and the gang.

Hearing our approach, Sam glanced over his shoulder. He was out of breath but grinning madly again.

"Gran got 'em!" he laughed, stepping to the side a pace so I could see.

Gloria Chalk was sitting astride her mobility scooter still, the helmet from a suit of armour on her head with the visor open. She held a huge sword in both hands – needed, I suspected, just to manage its weight. The sword's tip pressed against the professor's throat.

He was slumped against a wall, the fight taken out of him, but the craziest part of the whole scene was the rakish angle at which the scooter had come to rest.

I say come to rest because it was canted back at an angle supported underneath by Carlos' unconscious body. With the sword in her liver-spotted hands, it made Gloria look like she was a knight rearing a steed onto its hind legs. A yard away, the third henchman held his head where a nasty gash leaked blood over his fingers.

Was I supposed to laugh or cry?

I got to do neither due to the timely arrival of Captain Santoro and the Rio police. They burst into the museum's halls, barking orders, and pointing their flashlights.

They were not going to shoot us though. Thanks to Barbie and Hideki at the gate outside, the police knew what to expect. Well, I don't think any of them expected what they found, not even in their wildest dreams, but they secured the scene, disarming my team without feeling the need to liberally cuff us all just in case.

Captain Santoro came directly for me, his cheeks puffed out as he wrestled with what to say.

"Hello, Captain," I offered him my hand to shake.

He looked down at it and back up, giving me the sense that he was fighting an internal desire to throw me into jail regardless of the fact that I had been right all along.

Well, sort of.

He battled with himself for a two count, and just when I was going to lower my hand and berate him for being rude and ridiculous, he smacked his palm into mine.

"So, Mrs Fisher, I owe you an apology. Would you care to tell me what is going on here?"

"First things first, Sir." I angled my body to reveal Sonia Noriega. "This lady needs medical attention. She took a blow to the head and has been unconscious for more than a minute now. Also, there are two thugs in the basement. You'll want to dispatch some officers to collect them. They work for him," I pointed to Carlos. He was conscious again and displeased to be pinned beneath Gloria and her scooter.

"Anything else?" Captain Santoro tipped his head to the left, encouraging me to get it all out at once, with a subtext in his tone that I ought not to push my luck too far.

"Yes. We need to get back to our ship."

He choked on a laugh.

"Really, Mrs Fisher? You're serious? You bring down a gun battle in a museum in my town and think you can just stroll back to your ship so you can sail into the sunset five minutes later? There are forms to fill in. I need detailed statements from everyone."

"Well, if you want us to miss the ship and stay here in Rio ..."

Captain Santoro clicked his fingers. "Sergeant Braga, escort these civilians to the port and hurry up about it. Flashing lights, the full ensemble. Do not let them miss that boat!"

I had to laugh at the captain's urgency to get rid of us. He would have to explain to his bosses why he had let us go without recording statements and questioning us in detail, but it was clear which he preferred.

There was just one final item of business we needed to take care of.

Gin O'clock

We found Lieutenant Schneider in Professor Geller's office. He was none the worse for wear though angry as a bear that he'd been caught off guard the way he had. Back in the professor's office after the fake assault and robbery, he offered the unsuspecting security officer a drink. Whatever it was laced with had Schneider unconscious in seconds.

Schneider had no idea how long he'd been out for, but claimed he hadn't been awake for long. That meant he'd been out for at least six hours. Awaking to find a gag in his mouth, a canvas bag over his head, and both his hands and feet cable tied to the chair on which he sat, he tried calling for help, but couldn't make much noise and couldn't hear a sound to suggest there was anyone to hear him.

With the team reunited, we ran outside to find Barbie and Hideki.

They already knew we were fine through text messages from the team, but were relieved to see us all, nevertheless.

Unexpectedly, she had a message for me.

"The captain phoned ... Alistair, I mean, not the police captain. He has been trying to get a hold of you."

"Yeah, my phone got smashed." I showed her the remains which I had scooped before we left the basement room. "I don't think this is fixable."

Barbie agreed with her eyes, and said, "Well, the captain asked if you were done saving the world and would like to get back on the ship now. He'll be casting off soon."

In less than an hour, in fact and it was at least a half hour drive back to the ship. We had blown through the two hours I asked the chauffeurs to wait, but I spotted them both peering through the gates.

Drawn by the drama of flashing lights and shots being fired, they'd chosen to hang around so they would have a great story to tell in the morning.

We were in a hurry to get to them and be on our way, however a black car pulling up at the gates signalled another delay – Agent Patinkin had arrived. He was accompanied by several colleagues, at least two of whom I recognised from the industrial unit yesterday.

"Mrs Fisher," he called out even though I was already angling myself to meet him. "Congratulations."

I dipped my head. "Thank you. This was not exactly the outcome I was looking for. I came here to solve a murder and walked straight into an entirely different crime."

He wasn't here to see me, of course, I had busted a smuggling ring that he was supposed to be taking down - it was the local police and the scene inside the museum he came here for. His colleagues had already hustled by, heading toward the action, but since I had Agent Patinkin's attention, I threw a question his way.

"We got attacked and then shot at outside your little secret operations place yesterday afternoon. That wasn't your people, was it?"

He choked on a laugh and checked to see if I was being serious.

"No, Mrs Fisher. We heard the shots and looked outside to find four dead bodies lying in the street."

His news startled me. They were dead? We didn't kill them. That had to mean the fifth man did it. Was that accidental, like they got in the way when he was shooting at me? Or had I misconstrued the whole thing and he was always shooting at them, trying to protect some people he saw being attacked?

No, that didn't work because he then put three holes into the windscreen by Barbie's head.

"That shoot out and the bodies outside forced us to abandon our location, Mrs Fisher. The deaths were nothing to do with us."

Captain Santoro poked his head out of a museum window. "Mrs Fisher, what are you still doing here? Go to your ship before I change my mind!"

"I guess I had better get going," I mumbled, shaking Agent Patinkin's hand when he offered it in farewell.

With a pack of police cars cruising ahead, behind, and around us to make sure we could ignore all traffic signals and make haste to the port, we completed the journey in under twenty minutes. It had to be some kind of record.

Our chauffeur whooped when he went over a low rise in excess of seventy miles per hour and his wheels left the ground.

There were security officers waiting on the dockside for our arrival, urgently waving for us to get on board as the dock workers dealt with the ropes and such that held the ship in place. It was all such a frantic rush it felt as though we might have had to jump to get on board had we left it any later.

Out of breath, but with our heart rates returning to normal we waited just inside the royal suite's entrance for the elevator to descend.

No one spoke for a few moments, but my suggestion of, "Gin, anyone?" was greeted with a rousing round of approval.

In my suite a few moments later, the pace of our day ... our adventure in Rio finally slowed. The ship's mighty engines were running, sending an almost imperceptible vibration through its structure. We were bound for Miami, one of the few places on our trip that I had been to before.

Slumped in one corner of my couch with a pair of dachshunds curled into my lap, I had a cold glass of gin in my right hand and a room full of people I was glad to call friends.

Alistair would join me later, duties permitting, and that was okay because I was used to it.

Barbie was out of her wheelchair and sitting opposite me in a wing-back armchair. Hideki stood behind it, one arm draped over to hold Barbie's spare hand – her other held a glass of gin.

"Patty, what do we do about the treasure?" she asked.

"What do you mean?"

"Well," Barbie took a second to frame her thoughts. "You still have Finn Murphy's murder to solve. That's one thing and maybe it will remain unsolved, but someone broke in here and cracked your safe to steal the treasure. Not only that, someone else, who may or may not be connected to the man who broke in, pretended to be Professor Noriega, and came at us with a knife."

Jermaine joined in. "Then there were the men yesterday, madam."

Agent Patinkin had confirmed the men in the utility vehicle were nothing to do with him. Nor was the man who shot at me. Whoever that man was, he had to be connected to the giant I found in my suite because my handbag found its way back to me.

Neither Barbie nor Jermaine had posed a direct question, but I knew what they were asking – what was I going to do about it now?

I sipped some gin, revelling in the flavour and savouring the icy chill of it.

Looking up and around the room, everyone was waiting to hear my reply.

"I believe our knowledge of the treasure may still pose a threat to us all." I delivered what I believed was an honest answer and didn't sugar-coat it. "We don't know who the players are, but we do know they are prepared to kill to get what they are after. The only way for us to be sure we are safe might be to figure out where Finn Murphy found it."

"Find the treasure?" Sam wanted to clarify.

I nodded. "It's that or we sit back and hope the people who want it, who want to keep its existence a secret, don't come for us again."

I drained my glass and smiled at Jermaine – I needed another.

The End

Author's Note:

I t is a Tuesday afternoon in October as I write this little note. In nine days, I have my first proper vacation in three years. Like everyone else on the planet, my travel plans were put on hold by the global pandemic. We've had a few day trips and overnight stays in England this year, and I have been away as part of my work as an author, but as a family, this is essentially the first time my daughter has been anywhere.

I need to go back now and edit this book, the aim being to have it well and truly off my desk before I jet into the sunset with my suitcases. Like all my Patricia adventures, this one was fun to write, not least because I got to showcase Gloria more than in any prior book.

It may not be your experience, but to me, persons in the grandparenting age bracket have a tendency to act up. They might have been all for obeying the rules when they were younger, but they are less inclined now and employing experience as a marker for knowing what's best, they do as they choose.

Gloria is exactly like that; a nightmare to her children – Patricia plays the role of surrogate daughter - and nothing but entertainment for her grandchildren. I can assure you that it is nothing other than coincidence that I recently purchased a mobility scooter for my octogenarian mother.

It's purple.

This story features a character called Inigo Montoya. Some will have recognised the name instantly and responded by saying his most famous line. Inigo Montoya is a character in a 1973 book by William Goldman. The Princess Bride was also made into a film in which Inigo was brought to life by the American actor Mandy Patinkin. His line, which he continues saying while bleeding from a sword wound and refusing to give in, is, "My name is Inigo Montoya. You killed my father, prepare to die." And it's one of those movie moments that stuck, not only with me, but with many, many people.

Due to that, and because I like to slip in an occasional Easter egg, I took the name of the character and the actor who played him. Right now I am hoping the name isn't trademarked.

The sun is shining outside my window as I type the final words on novel seventy-six. It being October, it is both cool out, but warm in the sun. The leaves are fast losing their greenery though after the longest, hottest summer on record, the foliage in my garden was already looking a little wilted before the seasons changed.

In a few minutes, I have to leave my desk to attend a harvest festival celebration at my seven-year-old son's school. We live in a small village, nestled on a south-facing hillside and the school is probably less than a hundred yards from where I am currently sitting.

It was the opportunity to enjoy seeing my children grow that drove me to quit working for other people and strike out on my own. I have no regrets I can assure you, but circling back to the part about heading off on holiday ...

Before, a vacation was always something to look forward to, an opportunity to escape the daily grind. Not any longer. For the first time in my life, I am viewing the time away as a loss of working hours. I want to write books.

I don't want to write books more than I want to spend time with my family, but I will admit I find my priorities a tad confused today.

Between now and Christmas, I hope to commit at least three or four more stories to the page and will be starting a Blue Moon tale before I get on the flight. My good lady, Gemma, has already made it quite clear I will not spend the flight smashing words on my laptop as I would on a business trip.

Oh well.

Take care.

Steve Higgs

What's next for Patricia

With a billionaire about to get married onboard the Aurelia and a guest list that reads like a celebrity who's who, tension among the security team is understandably high.

They are being extra vigilant, but that doesn't stop the bride-to-be receiving a death threat if she dares to go through with the ceremony.

So who sent it and is the threat genuine?

Could it be from one of the groom's four ex-wives? None were invited, yet they all turned up and while there is no love between them, they appear to be plotting.

It's Patricia's job to figure things out and she is glad for every bit of help she can get.

Thankfully old friend and celebrity wedding planner, Felicity Philips, is there to lend a hand even if her sleuthing skills are a little … questionable.

Determined to get to the bottom of the mystery before it impacts the wedding ceremony, Patricia is soon thrown off course when a murder occurs.

With a celebrity columnist on the ship stirring things up in the hope of a winning headline, the bride's skanky family looking for a fast score, and the ship crawling with more celebrities than a red carpet in Hollywood Patricia has her work cut out.

Oh, and Lady Mary is back, so that will help … not!

Pets Investigate

Sticking their noses where they are most definitely not wanted.

Despairing of their humans, these pets take it upon themselves to solve the cases they see as only cats and dogs can.

Whether they sniff out the clues or fool the criminals into thinking they are harmless pets to be ignored, Rex, Amber, Buster, and more enjoy escapades a-plenty in this fun collection of short stories.

Grab your copy and be ready for the fur to fly!

<u>**More Books By Steve Higgs**</u>

Blue Moon Investigations
Paranormal Nonsense
The Phantom of Barker Mill
Amanda Harper Paranormal Detective
The Klowns of Kent
Dead Pirates of Cawsand
In the Doodoo With Voodoo
The Witches of East Malling
Crop Circles, Cows and Crazy Aliens
Whispers in the Rigging
Bloodlust Blonde – a short story
Paws of the Yeti
Under a Blue Moon – A Paranormal
Detective Origin Story
Night Work
Lord Hale's Monster
The Herne Bay Howlers
Undead Incorporated
The Ghoul of Christmas Past
The Sandman
Jailhouse Golem
Shadow in the Mine
Ghost Writer

Felicity Philips Investigates
To Love and to Perish
Tying the Noose
Aisle Kill Him
A Dress to Die For
Wedding Ceremony Woes

Patricia Fisher Cruise Mysteries
The Missing Sapphire of Zangrabar
The Kidnapped Bride
The Director's Cut
The Couple in Cabin 2124
Doctor Death
Murder on the Dancefloor
Mission for the Maharaja
A Sleuth and her Dachshund in Athens
The Maltese Parrot
No Place Like Home

Patricia Fisher Mystery Adventures
What Sam Knew
Solstice Goat
Recipe for Murder
A Banshee and a Bookshop
Diamonds, Dinner Jackets, and Death
Frozen Vengeance
Mug Shot
The Godmother
Murder is an Artform
Wonderful Weddings and Deadly
Divorces
Dangerous Creatures

Patricia Fisher: Ship's Detective Series
The Ship's Detective
Fitness Can Kill
Death by Pirates
First Dig Two Graves

Albert Smith Culinary Capers
Pork Pie Pandemonium
Bakewell Tart Bludgeoning
Stilton Slaughter
Bedfordshire Clanger Calamity
Death of a Yorkshire Pudding
Cumberland Sausage Shocker
Arbroath Smokie Slaying
Dundee Cake Dispatch
Lancashire Hotpot Peril
Blackpool Rock Bloodshed
Kent Coast Oyster Obliteration
Eton Mess Massacre
Cornish Pasty Conspiracy

Realm of False Gods
Untethered magic
Unleashed Magic
Early Shift
Damaged but Powerful
Demon Bound
Familiar Territory
The Armour of God
Live and Die by Magic
Terrible Secrets

About the Author

At school, the author was mostly disinterested in every subject except creative writing, for which, at age ten, he won his first award. However, calling it his first award suggests that there have been more, which there have not. Accolades may come but, in the meantime, he is having a ball writing mystery stories and crime thrillers and claims to have more than a hundred books forming an unruly queue in his head as they clamour to get out. He lives in the south-east corner of England with a duo of lazy sausage dogs. Surrounded by rolling hills, brooding castles, and vineyards, he doubts he will ever leave, the beer is just too good.

If you are a social media fan, you should copy the link below into your browser to join my very active Facebook group. You'll find a host of friends waiting there, some of whom have been with me from the very start.

My Facebook group get first notification when I publish anything new, plus cover reveals and free short stories, but more than that, they all interact with each other, sharing inside jokes, and answering question.

f facebook.com/stevehiggsauthor

You can also keep updated with my books via my website:

g https://stevehiggsbooks.com/